THE COUPLE IN THE CABIN

DANIEL HURST

www.danielhurstbooks.com

Download My Free Book

If you would like to receive a FREE copy of my psychological thriller 'Just One Second', then you can find the link to the book at my website www.danielhurstbooks.com

PROLOGUE

A sturdy, wooden cabin standing at the bottom of a well-maintained garden at the rear of a large property in the English countryside. Sounds nice, doesn't it?

But what if there was more to the cabin than first meets the eye?

The cabin itself had cost quite a lot of money, but like any man-made structure, it was all about the story behind it rather than the nuts and bolts that went into its construction.

The cabin belonged to Dominic Brown. It had been his idea to have it built, his time spent talking to the builders, and his money used to fund the project. It would also be used predominantly by him. But before all of that, he had needed permission, and that had to come from his wife, Grace.

Dominic had raised the idea of building a cabin in the couple's spacious back garden by suggesting it would be the perfect place for him to 'work from home', away from the noise and distractions in the house and somewhere he could leave his paperwork without frustrating his partner, who was forever telling him to try and be a little tidier. While that idea was met with some enthusiasm by Grace, she was less impressed when she learned how much the whole thing would cost.

The cabin wasn't going to just be some shoddy structure thrown together cheaply. No, Dominic wanted it to be state-of-the-art. It needed electricity so that he could go online while inside it. It needed a heater so that he could stay warm while working there in winter. And he wanted it to be big enough so that he didn't feel cramped. Enough room for a desk and chair but also enough room for him to stand up fully, really stretch his legs, feel at home. And maybe even space for a TV and dartboard for the moments he needed to relax.

Grace had to ask him if this was really a place for him to work or a place for him to escape for a little 'alone time', but Dominic insisted everything that he required was for purely professional reasons. And he also insisted on having all the amenities he described, well aware it would be expensive, but he had a good job, and he didn't spend a lot of money in other ways, so why couldn't he allow himself this luxury?

To Grace, this seemed like it might be a mid-life crisis manifesting itself in her husband in a rather unusual way. Some men who entered their forties and were struck down with creeping fears about their mortality were suddenly compelled to go and spend big money on something that made them feel young again, if not look it. Traditionally, it was a sports car, although it could be anything really, from new and flashy clothes to new and flashy teeth, the kind that could be seen from quite a distance away on a dark night. Whatever it was, the point was that it was supposed to make the person feel better about the fact that they were now potentially halfway through their existence on this planet, and the last remnants of their youth were nothing but a distant dream.

Was the cabin Dominic's way of expressing his fear of death? Was it his one shot at cheering himself up and distracting himself from what lay ahead? Or, like the sports cars, the suits and the teeth that so many men had before him, was it just going to prove to be yet another expensive waste of money?

Grace had her doubts, financially and philosophically, but in the end, she agreed to her husband's idea to build a cabin in the back garden.

With that seal of approval issued, she had left him to deal with all the issues around planning permission, which was a legal requirement. She also left him to notify the next-door neighbours that there would be some disruption for a short while when the building work started, which was not required by law but was more a gesture of goodwill. Fortunately for Dominic, and perhaps unfortunately for Grace, the neighbours had no objection, and the couple next door, Frank and Maggie, even thought it was a good idea and wondered if they should do the same themselves in their own garden. That was the thing with this area. The houses were big, the land was plentiful, and the residents often had more money than sense.

Dominic was like a child on Christmas morning when his cabin was eventually finished, and he quickly set to work filling it with all the things he had dreamt about. The only thing he regretted was not having space for a small fridge in which he could have stored a few beers, but that wasn't the end of the world. It was only a short walk through the garden back to the main house whenever he got thirsty.

With his new 'office' established, Dominic worked out of it four days a week, only having to leave it on occasion when he was required to go to his real office in town and liaise with his colleagues face to face instead of through his laptop screen. But he also found time to go in the cabin on the weekends, making some excuse about 'some paperwork that needed completing', but really, he just liked to go inside, close the door, turn on the TV and have a little peace.

He was a couple of decades away from retirement yet, just like his wife was, but this cabin was definitely somewhere he felt he would spend even more time once he did leave the world of employment behind. Little did he know just how much time he would be spending in the cabin after things went so horribly wrong for him in the near future.

But go wrong they did.

The cabin that was once so pristine and perfect and the pride and joy of its owner eventually became the symbol of everything that was wrong between Grace and Dominic.

On the day the police came, all of that important paperwork that Dominic used to store so neatly in trays and folders was strewn around the cabin, discarded and, in some cases, destroyed. A broken wine bottle lay on the desk, its sharp edges a hazard to anyone who went near them, not to mention the several shards of glass on the wooden floor that were a danger to tread on. And there was even blood in there, the red dots scattered across the white paper on the floor, possibly from a cut caused by the glass, but potentially from something else.

Something worse.

The cabin looked like a warzone. Something truly terrible had happened in there. And it was up to the police to figure it all out.

Sure, the cabin at the bottom of the garden might have been a good idea at one time.

But in the end, it became nothing more than a crime scene.

And worse than that, it became the place where Grace and Dominic really learnt the truth about one another.

BEFORE THE POLICE CAME

1

GRACE

I'm in a stranger's car. A man I met only three hours ago is driving me home. For me, this is very spontaneous. But it's not what you think. I haven't found myself a lover, and I'm not rushing headfirst into a one-night stand. What exists between me and the man at the wheel is nothing but polite friendship, and it's a friendship that started back at the bar we have just left.

There I was, standing around with several of my colleagues making small talk at our employer's latest and rather boring 'networking' event, when I had started to wonder if I'd made a mistake in agreeing to book myself a hotel room for the night instead of just going home after my professional duties were complete.

My boss had given us all the option to stay in the hotel next to the bar at the company's expense, and not one to turn down a freebie, I had gratefully accepted. So had several of my colleagues, and with us all planning on a late one, it seemed like a fun night ahead beckoned. But I'd quickly realised that I wasn't twenty-one anymore. Nor was I even thirty-one. I'm forty-one, so a late night out socialising and staying away from home was not quite as exciting as it once was.

That had left me fearing that I'd been too quick to take the opportunity of a free hotel room, and I had found myself thinking about my husband at home and how I'd much prefer to be getting into bed with him tonight instead of being alone. I've been married to my partner, Dominic, for eleven years, and in all that time, I'd say we've only spent a dozen or so nights apart. Most of them have come recently too, the result of one of us having to work late, mainly him, or attend some corporate event, much like the one I was at tonight.

We both work 9-5 office type jobs, or 'pushing papers' as my grandfather would have called it, but he was a construction worker, so anything that didn't result in muddy clothes and calloused hands didn't seem like a job to him. The only difference in terms of work between Dominic and I is my employers still have the quite archaic rule of their employees being in the office every day, whereas Dominic's have moved more with the times and allowed him to complete the majority of his professional duties from the comfort of his own home. There wasn't much to thank the recent pandemic for, but as my husband puts it, "it's changed the world forever, and one of those ways is that people can now hold meetings in their pyjamas."

Neither Dominic nor I earn mega money for what we do, but I still consider us to be fairly affluent for our age, a result of us choosing not to have children, which is certainly the cheapest option, and a few generous inheritances that have come to us after we sadly said goodbye to a few cherished family members over the years. My beloved grandfather, who was my mother's dad and the one who worked so long in construction, left me a sizeable sum, proving how much he loved me, not that I ever felt like I needed proof to know it. And Dominic's grandparents very kindly left him money too, funds that can't ever replace the people who gave them but certainly helped us buy our current home, a place we would never have been able to afford before.

We are the owners of a beautiful property that has everything I suspect most people dream about in a house, and that would be *space*. Spare bedrooms. Spare bathrooms. Spare cupboards in the kitchen. And plenty of spare room in the garden, although a big portion of that was quickly filled by a wood cabin that I'm still not convinced about and doubt I ever will be.

But there's more to life than just houses and money. I know the thing that makes it worth living are the people, and with Dominic, I've found myself a good man. A loyal, loving and funny companion who I am very much looking forward to growing old with. But it was the thoughts of my man that had continued to dominate my thinking at the work event, and no amount of free champagne and friendly chats with the people I was with were making up for it.

And then I met Clark.

I was introduced to him by Kelly, my colleague, who always takes networking opportunities seriously and had been wandering around the bar chatting to both our current clients and the potential clients that I probably should have been talking to myself.

'He's from your side of town,' Kelly had told me, handing over her business card to the man she had just introduced me to before walking away as if she had just acted as a kind of matchmaker, although in this case, it was more about getting sales than getting physical.

I didn't want to be rude, so I made conversation, picking up on the loose thread my colleague had left me hanging with by asking Clark exactly whereabouts in town he was from.

'I live on Foundation Street,' he had told me. 'The nice end, not the end with all the trouble, although the trouble seems to be creeping closer by the day.'

I'd smiled at that and told him I knew where he meant, although I didn't mention that I only knew because I'd heard the street name on the news a couple of times in relation to a few burglaries that had taken place. Then he'd asked me where I lived, and I'd found myself feeling like I needed to downplay it somewhat.

'Oh, I'm just on Royal Lane. But we get some trouble too. I don't think there's anywhere in this town that is crime-free anymore, is there?'

I'd been exaggerating there because my part of town was actually completely crime-free, more out of sheer luck than thanks to any kind of neighbourhood watch scheme. The fact that there were only a few houses on Royal Lane, and they were all out in the countryside, meant that presumably, they weren't as easy to get to for would-be burglars as more residential streets like where Clark lived. But he'd seen through my attempt at being polite rather easily.

'Ahh, I'd always wondered who lived in those houses,' he had mused. 'Or rather, I'd always wondered who I should be envious of.'

I'd chuckled at that before I'd moved the conversation on quickly there, not wanting to make him any more jealous of where I lived than he already was. Seeing as it was supposed to be a work event, I'd steered us onto the topic of what we did in our respective roles.

It had turned out that he was a Seller, which was handy because I was a Buyer, so we'd talked about the possible ways our respective employers could work together for a while, before he'd quite rightly stated that the last thing anybody wanted to do at one of these kinds of events was actually talk about work.

We'd chatted about more interesting things then, from where we went on our last holidays to whether or not the free champagne that we were all drinking was cheap or actually quite decent. He told me that he was back from a recent trip to Italy, while I mentioned I'd been over to Greece in the summer. And we both agreed that the champagne was not that bad, actually.

I'd been enjoying Clark's company and had also respected the fact that he hadn't tried getting flirty with me, even though he was of a similar age to me, and I saw no wedding ring on his left hand. That was why I hadn't baulked completely when he offered me a lift home only a moment after I had told him how I was regretting agreeing to stay out.

'Oh, no, you don't need to do that,' I'd told him. 'I'll probably just stay in the hotel. It seems silly to waste the booking.'

'I'm sure your manager won't mind. They'll never know if you don't use the room.'

'True. But if I do decide to go home, I'll be fine getting a taxi.'

'No problem. But like I say, I'll be going that way on my way home, so I'm happy to drop you off. Just let me know. I'll probably leave in half an hour or so.'

Clark had smiled at me then before wandering over to a buffet table and helping himself to a couple of the canapes that I had been avoiding all night on account of how many calories I imagined they contained. From there, I'd tried to forget all about him and the offer he had made me as I'd gone back to chatting with a few of my co-workers, but as the minutes had ticked by, I'd found myself keeping an eye on him for fear of losing sight of him in the crowd.

After all, he was my ticket home.

I knew that all I had to do was tell him I'd accept the offer of a ride, and I could be back in my own house in my own bed very shortly. It was either that or stand outside and try to get a taxi, something that could be easier said than done in this town that hasn't accepted Uber yet and had instead stuck stubbornly with the local firms who seem to regard passengers as inconveniences rather than customers. If not that then it was the lonely hotel room for me. Not great options, and all reasons why I kept thinking about Clark and the offer of a free ride.

Having considered it some more, I'd figured that it was surely better for me to get in a car with someone who I'd been talking to and getting along with rather well as opposed to an unfamiliar taxi driver. And better to go home than spend all night in a very unfamiliar hotel room. So that was my mind made up.

In the end, I'd given my excuses to my colleagues about having to leave early, stuffed a couple of the naughty canapes into my mouth because I hadn't been able to resist them forever, and then gone to Clark and told him I'd love to hitch a ride with him if his offer still stood. And to justify my decision a little more and alleviate some of my guilt about leaving this work event earlier, I'd told him he was to come to my office and pitch me on what he was selling some time soon, so at least my boss would think I had actually done some valuable networking after all.

He'd smiled and finished his mineral water then before we'd left the bar, and after I'd taken my spot on his passenger seat in a rather nice car that made me think he was better at his job than he had been letting on, we'd been on our way. Now, after many left and right turns on the country lanes near my home, we're about five minutes out from my house, and the journey has been a pleasant one. The conversation has been just as natural and free-flowing between us as it had been back at the bar, and the further we get away from that busy, noisy venue, the more I was glad I'd taken a chance and seized my opportunity to come home after all.

I know Dominic will be surprised to see me when I get back. I'd made it clear that I would be away all night, and I've never been one for changing plans at the last minute, so there's no way he would expect me to be as unpredictable as to walk through the front door when I shouldn't do. But I have been, and while I'm tempted to text him and tell him that I'm about to arrive back unexpectedly, I decide not to because I'm mischievously curious about what he might be up to while he thinks he has the house to himself.

Then again, my husband has never been particularly unpredictable either.

While some wives might worry about walking in unexpectedly on their partner and finding them up to something naughty, I don't have that worry myself. That's because I know exactly what my husband will be doing. He'll be in the cabin in our back garden, the one he so passionately insisted that he needed to have constructed so that he had somewhere quiet to work during the week. That pile of wood cost us a small fortune, almost as much as an actual brick-and-mortar extension on our house, but to Dominic, it was money well spent because he's barely left the place since it was built. I bet he's in there right now, sitting in his armchair in front of the small TV he insisted on having in there, a cold beer in one hand and the remote control in the other. To me, that would hardly be making the most of having the whole house to himself, but then again, Dominic has everything he needs in that cabin of his.

I can't help but smile to myself as I think about how he's such a simple man. I suppose I should be glad he isn't always talking about wanting exotic holidays or feeling a yearning to uproot our lives with some silly adventure designed for people half our age. He's happy just to sit at the bottom of the garden and have some peace and quiet, and as much as I tease him about that fact, I love him for it too.

'Which one is it?' Clark asks me as he slows down and peers out through the windscreen at the row of dark houses ahead of us, and I realise that we're back already. That was much quicker than a taxi would have been, and it came with none of the usual dodgy smells either.

'The one on the left,' I tell him, pointing the way. 'But anywhere around here is fine. Thank you very much.'

I remove my seatbelt and pick up my handbag from the footwell as he brings the car to a stop, and he makes sure to give me his business card before wishing me a good evening. I take the card and thank him again before I exit the vehicle, and as I prepare to go inside, I feel like all is well with the world.

But it's not.

Far from it.

Things are about to get very crazy, very fast.

2

DOMINIC

'You know, I was just thinking. I'm pretty sure we've now had sex in every room in this house.'

I smile at the words the woman in my arms has just said, before sniffing her hair and kissing her head.

'You know, I think you might be right,' I reply, trying not to sound too smug about it, but it's impossible not to feel at least a little pleased with myself. Any man who gets to be intimate with a woman like Kamilla, my saucy mistress, is a lucky one, but a man who gets to be intimate with her in several places?

That's more than lucky.

'All the bedrooms. The bathrooms. The kitchen. The dining room. And now the living room. Yep, I think that's all of them,' she says, nodding after she has ticked them all off in her mind.

'Which was your favourite?' I ask her, cheekily curious.

'Hmm. It has to be the kitchen. Those countertops were the perfect height. You?'

'I liked the bathroom. That was the best shower I've ever had.'

Kamilla laughs at my answer while I momentarily lose myself in a daydream about that steamy shower the pair of us shared a few weeks ago on another night when my wife was out of the house.

My wife.

Grace. My other half. The woman I'm cheating on.

I do feel bad about it, of course I do. Guilt. Remorse. Shame. Yep, I feel it all. But even with all that, I still can't stop myself. I can't stop seeing Kamilla, and I haven't been able to do so ever since I met her.

My fairly boring job is one I can do mostly from home, but the odd time I am required to go to the office every week ended up resulting in a chance encounter with a woman who would change my life rather unexpectedly. I suppose one could say I was sleepwalking through my existence before I met Kamilla. Going through the motions. Just doing what I was expected to do. But then I encountered her, and everything changed. It was like I'd been reawakened and reminded that there could be more exciting things in the world than getting to watch a little television before bed. Before her, the building of my cabin in the garden was the most exhilarating thing that had happened to me in a long time, and that's saying something.

We met as we crossed paths in the office one quiet Tuesday morning. I'd immediately clocked the attractive blonde heading my way and knew I'd never seen her in my workplace before, so I'd tried to stay cool before I smiled and asked her if she was new. She told me that she was and explained that she had just joined the company as a 'temp'. That meant her employment was not permanent. It was casual, flexible and open to all sorts of possibilities.

Everything my eleven-year marriage was not.

We chatted for a little while as I welcomed Kamilla to the company and told her that she shouldn't hesitate to ask me if she needed any help with anything. She had thanked me and told me I was very kind before we had separated, and I'd gone on with my day, not thinking any more about it. Okay, that's a bit of a lie. I'd found myself thinking about Kamilla a lot after our meeting, although mainly in the form of wistful daydreams that I presumed would never amount to much.

That was until she started emailing me and asking me for all sorts of things.

At first, I thought she was genuinely curious about the new company she had joined and was taking me up on my offer of help, but after several messages back and forth between us, it became clear she was just looking for any excuse to keep in contact with me. However, I was hardly going to complain about having the attention of a pretty woman, so I made sure to keep replying, and pretty quickly, our correspondence became less formal and a little flirtier.

As well as being unexpected, another thing the emails did was keep me entertained while I sat in my cabin for most of the week, removed from the rest of the world. The messages also made me eagerly anticipate the one day a week I got to go into the office and see her, and once there, Kamilla and I only grew closer.

It was during one of those times that she had offered to buy me a drink to thank me for all the help and advice I had been giving her over email, and I'd jumped at the chance. I still felt like nothing would happen because this was real-life, not a movie, but one drink turned into several, and before I knew it, I was locking lips with a woman half my age.

Did I mention Kamilla was only twenty-four?

Not bad for a man in his forties, hey?

Of course it's wrong. Of course I shouldn't have become involved with a woman who wasn't my wife. But it happened, and it has continued to happen, and I can't quite see how I'm ever going to be able to bring myself to stop, especially not when she keeps talking about all the rooms in the house where she blew my mind.

'What about doing it in the back garden?' she asks me then, once again surprising me with her sense of adventure. Grace can barely bring herself to be intimate with me under the duvet on our bed on my birthday, yet here is Kamilla suggesting we get physical on the lawn beneath nothing but the stars in the sky. But while I'm clearly a risk taker, considering the secretive affair I have embarked on, outdoors sex does seem a little too adventurous even for me.

'I'm not sure. I just put some treatment on the grass last week, and it might irritate our skin,' I tell Kamilla, and she laughs before saying that it was a very 'old man' response.

I feign hurt, even though I'm actually not, because while she jokes about my age quite often, I've figured out by now that she clearly has a thing for more senior men, so me being two decades older than her is really not a problem in her eyes. And it's certainly not a problem in mine.

'Hmm, I'm just trying to think of somewhere new we could do it,' she goes on as she runs her hands across my bare chest. 'I wouldn't want things to get stale between us.'

The very mention of the word 'stale' is a call-back to how I've described my marriage to her several times, but it's also a hint from my mistress that she likes things to be fun and random, so me choosing to play it safe might not be my best way of keeping her interested in the long run. That's why I rack my brains for somewhere else we could be physical where we haven't been before.

And then I have it.

'You know, we haven't done it in my cabin,' I tell her. 'That's technically in the garden.'

Kamilla lifts her head up then and looks at me, clearly interested in what I've just said.

'Then what are we waiting for? Let's go, big boy!'

She takes me by the hand and leads me to the door, and even though I suggest we slow down a little bit so we can put a few clothes on before we go outside, she has no interest in covering up. To be fair, we need to be naked for what we are planning to do, so I guess it doesn't make sense to get dressed as that would only waste time. I also know that my back garden isn't overlooked by any of my neighbours' houses, so I don't have to worry about being spotted scampering across my lawn, naked as the day I was born, with an equally naked woman who is definitely not Grace. The closest neighbours to me are Frank and Maggie next door, but they'll both be inside now, most likely sitting in front of the TV because just like my marriage, theirs is depressingly predictable too.

Feeling as energetic as a man half my age, I unlock the back door and instantly feel the cold air on my bare skin as I step outside. Instinctively, my hands go over my groin to cover my modesty, as well as keep me warm, but Kamilla has no such problem with moving freely, and she almost skips into my back garden as she moves in the direction of the cabin.

I'm just about to close the back door before I follow her, but before I do, I grab the key to the cabin from its hook as well as the half-full bottle of wine from the kitchen counter. I also make sure to steal a glance at the clock on the wall in my kitchen and when I do, I see that it says half-past ten.

The night is still reasonably young, and Grace is staying in a hotel this evening, so she won't be back until tomorrow. That means I've still got several enjoyable hours in Kamilla's company yet.

And I intend to make the most of every second.

Closing the door behind me, I see Kamilla is already waiting down by the cabin, and she whispers to me to hurry up as I notice her start to shiver. I appreciate her keeping her voice down because while Frank and Maggie won't be able to see us in my garden, they could hear us if they have any of their windows open.

I jog across the lawn with the wine bottle in hand, my bare feet sinking easily into the grass as I go before I reach the cabin and put the key in the lock. I hadn't been planning on coming in here again until tomorrow morning when another day of work was due to begin, but I can't say I'm disappointed to be entering now.

'So, this is where you spend most of your time, is it?' Kamilla says as we step into my cabin and I feel the wooden floorboards beneath my feet. 'It's quite roomy, isn't it?'

'Yeah, it's great,' I tell her, feeling proud of my creation. I wish Grace was as enthusiastic about this place as Kamilla seems to be. Then again, Grace only sees this cabin as a sort of 'man cave'. My mistress, on the other hand, sees this place as something that both a male and a female can very much enjoy together, and she proves it by grabbing me and pulling me in further.

The cabin door is still ajar as we tumble down onto the rug that offers a little more comfort than the wooden boards it sits upon, but neither of us are thinking about closing that door as we pick up where we left off in the house.

I wish we had been.

I wish we had stopped and thought about things for a second.

If so, it would have spared both of us everything that was to come next.

3

GRACE

I unlock the front door to my house and step inside, trying to be quiet in case Dominic is already upstairs asleep. It's late enough for him to have perhaps called it a night, and I don't want to wake him if he is resting. But all the lights are still on in the house, so I'm guessing he's still up somewhere.

I hope, for his sake, he is because if he is in bed, I'll be giving him a telling off for wasting electricity.

I close the door quietly as I hear the low rumble of Clark's car engine driving away in the distance, thinking as I do about what a gentleman he was and how the world isn't quite as full of bad men as some people might have you think. Then I hang my coat on the hook beside my husband's and kick off my heels, instantly feeling the soothing fresh air on my aching ankles after several hours spent tottering around in my tight-fitting footwear.

My plan now is to quickly find Dominic and update him about how my night went before I grab a glass of water from the kitchen and get into bed because I have work duties to report for in the morning and don't want to be too tired. But no sooner have I started moving through my home then I start to detect that things might not be right around here.

The first thing that confuses me is the sight of the bra lying on the living room floor.

I don't recognise it, and after picking it up and checking the fabric, I know for certain that it is not one of mine.

So whose is it?

The bra isn't the only item of clothing in here. I see a t-shirt too, one that I know belongs to Dominic because I've put it in the washing machine countless times. It's strewn across one arm of the sofa, not far from a black sock and a belt I recognise as one I bought for my husband last Christmas.

What is going on? Why does it look like Dominic got undressed in a hurry?

And who the hell does this damn bra belong to?

I call out to my husband then, no longer worrying whether or not he might be asleep, but I get no response. All I get is more of a mystery as I walk into other rooms and find more clothing.

A white blouse that isn't mine. Another black sock. And then I see the pair of shoes lying near the kitchen door, a set of heels that I would never wear, mainly because I definitely wouldn't be able to walk in them. They belong to another woman, just like the bra and the blouse, and there's probably a pair of knickers around here too belonging to her if I look hard enough.

It's becoming obvious to me now what is going on here.

Dominic has another woman in our house.

'No, this can't be,' I whisper, the sound of my voice so low in this quiet house, but it's all the volume I can muster at this time as I process the shock of coming home and making a discovery like this.

I never, ever, for one second in my marriage, considered that such a thing might happen to me. Dominic is a good man. A good husband. *Or at least I thought he was until thirty seconds ago.*

It takes all my strength just to keep my body from shaking as an awful cocktail of fear, panic, heartbreak and nausea swirls around inside of me.

'Dominic! Where are you?' I cry, feeling hurt but there's an anger bubbling to the surface now. It's only simmering but the longer this goes, the more I feel like it will boil over.

I head for the staircase and take the steps two at a time while still holding the mystery bra, the lacy fabric between my fingers, the straps hanging down beside me, brushing my skin, making it turn colder by the second.

I'm guessing they're both in the bedroom. Two lovers entangled in the sheets. Having fun. Laughing at my expense. But they won't be laughing when I walk in and catch them in the act.

What will I do when I get there?

Scream? Shout? Attack?

I guess I'll just do whatever feels right in the moment and deal with the consequences afterwards.

But to my surprise, not to mention a little relief, the bed is empty. There's not any sign that the duvet has been disturbed. They aren't in here. Nor are they in the ensuite bathroom or any of the spare bedrooms.

It seems that the whole house is clear, and if it wasn't for the clothes everywhere, I wouldn't know anybody had been here at all. But they clearly have been. Dominic has been here, and he has a mystery guest, one who clearly likes to unburden herself from having to wear clothes.

So where are they?

I pace around the various rooms, retracing my steps, my feet digging into the carpet and my fists clenched as I search for the lovers, but as I do, there is a brief moment when I have the possibly naïve idea that things might not be as bad as they seem here.

What if there is another explanation for this? What if my husband isn't with another woman? What if the items of female clothing I have found are his?

What if he is one of those men that likes to dress up as a woman in secret?

It's silly, but I'm actually holding out hope that it might be the explanation for all of this. It would be very weird if my husband was a cross-dresser and would require us to have a bit of a serious conversation about it, but it would be far preferable to him turning out to be an adulterer.

Please let that be it, I think to myself as I keep looking for him. *Please let this be anything other than what I fear it is.*

Still no nearer to getting any answers, I try and fathom why, if Dominic is having an affair, he seems to have left the evidence all over the place for me to find. I didn't have to be Sherlock Holmes to stumble upon and decipher this crime scene, after all. Could he really have been so brazen as to have a woman here, engage in intercourse and then go out for a while, leaving the mess behind? But then I remember that he would have believed that I wouldn't be home until tomorrow, so I guess that explains his boldness. But even so, this does seem a little careless of him to leave all this stuff here.

Unless he is still around somewhere.

He might not be in the house.

But he might be in the back garden.

I rush to our bedroom window and look out and when I do, I can just make out the shape of the cabin in the darkness. Another one of the annoying things about it is that it's always the first thing I see when I open the curtains in the morning and look outside. But right now, it gives me the chance to see if there is any activity down there, and the sight of the half-open cabin door suggests I have just located my missing man.

He's in there.

But is he alone?

Despite desperately wanting to know the answer to that question, I move slowly as I go downstairs, my legs trembling beneath me because I fear I'm on the verge of everything falling apart. If Dominic is up to something he shouldn't be then there's nothing he can do to cover it up now, so I don't need to rush.

I had the element of surprise the moment I decided to come home early.

Now I just need to try and keep the element of control.

I step out into the back garden and glare at the cabin, the sight of it tormenting me even more so than usual. First it took lots of money, then it took lots of space and now, it might just be about to take my marriage too.

I walk towards it, my feet on the grass and my eyes on the open door, and as I get nearer, I start to hear things.

Heavy breathing.

A giggle.

And then a moan.

Unfortunately, only one of those sounds seemed to come from my husband. The latter two were most definitely made by a female, and despite still being a few yards away from the cabin, I already know what I am going to see once I look inside it.

My brain quickly offers me a way out to avoid the trauma of this situation, suggesting to me that I just go back inside and act as if nothing is happening. I could even gather up my belongings and leave the house, calling a taxi to take me back to the bar and spend the night in the hotel I should have stayed in all along. If I do that then Dominic will never know that I was here, and I don't have to face the fact that my husband is a cheat.

Play dumb. Act. Forget.

But that's impossible.

I can't run from this any more than my husband can.

Reaching the doorway, the moaning grows louder, and I grit my teeth as I grip the door handle and look inside.

And there they both are.

Naked.

Him on top of her.

Whoever she is.

My God, she looks young. Is she in her twenties? Maybe. She's definitely blonde, and that stings because Dominic always told me he was a brunette guy. The liar. But that's clearly not all he's lied about. He's lied to me about everything and made a fool out of me in the process.

But he still hasn't seen me. Neither has she. His young, energetic mistress. Both their eyes are closed as they kiss while their bodies move in sync, showcasing a rhythm that me and Dominic have not displayed since the early years of our relationship.

I thought the days of my husband being so passionate were long gone. Little did I know he just needed the right partner to be passionate with. I guess I couldn't bring it out of him, but this woman clearly can.

Is this my fault? Did I not show him enough affection? Did I not keep him happy? Am I the bad guy here?

No, of course not. I'm the loyal wife who has stayed faithful.

And he's the dirty pig who has just broken my heart.

It's as if he can somehow hear my heartstrings being pulled apart inside my chest at that moment because Dominic suddenly opens his eyes and looks back towards the doorway, and when he does, he gets the shock of his life.

'Grace!' he cries breathlessly, and his sweaty, naked torso stops moving then, just like the torso beneath him stops wriggling too.

Two sets of eyes are on me, those of my husband and his mistress.

Both caught in the act.

Both vulnerable.

Both unable to explain things.

And after I quickly close the door and turn the key, *both locked in the cabin.*

4

DOMINIC

How has this happened?

How have I been caught?

'Grace! Wait, I can explain!' I cry as I get off Kamilla and rush to the door, grabbing the handle and trying to pull it open. But the door is locked. Grace must have turned the key. That means we're trapped in here now.

But she has to let me out.

She has to let me tell her that this isn't what she thinks it is.

That's when I realise the absurdity of the situation. How my wife just caught me naked with another woman in the cabin in our back garden. A woman I shouldn't be with, in a cabin I begged to have built. There's no possible way I can talk my way out of this. No feeble excuse I can offer. Not any way I can say "it's not how it looks."

The reality of it is as clear as day.

I've been having an affair, and now I've been rumbled.

What will Grace do now? Will she divorce me? Take half my money? Leave me stuck on the fringes of society, one of those despicable divorcees who cheated, lost everything and ends up living alone in some crummy bedsit with nobody to visit him because he ruined every relationship he ever had with his nonsensical, morally corrupt behaviour?

Oh God, is that my fate? I doubt Kamilla would come and visit me if so. She's been happy to come here, to this big house, but she might not be so happy to see me in whatever awful place I end up living in after the divorce lawyers have got their claws stuck into me and my finances. I've heard the horror stories of how expensive marital separations can be. Now I'm going to be one of the statistics. A loser. I'll certainly lose both of them, my wife and my mistress, but the fact I even have two women to consider tells me everything I need to know about how much I deserve this.

I've been a fool. I had a good woman. I had it all. Sure, it was boring, but it was safe. But I risked it all for an adventure with a young woman who will probably just find another older guy to take my place, one who hasn't had his bank account emptied by a vengeful ex.

'Grace, open the door!'

Fear, panic and anxiety threaten to get the better of me as I try to plead my case, but rather here than in a mediation meeting that's billable by the hour.

'Grace! Come on, unlock this door, please! We need to talk!'

That last part is an understatement. We do need to talk, or rather I need to talk. I need to find a stream of words that will make her not hate me as much as she surely does right now. Some assortment of letters uttered in the right order that will make her not despise my being and feel the need to punish me even more.

I'd tell her that I made a mistake. I'm an idiot. A fool. A man who lost his mind for the briefest of moments but a man who can change. A man who can be forgiven.

Forgiveness. That's what I need now.

But I can't get it while I'm stuck in here.

'Grace! Please! Open the door!'

I keep calling to my wife, but she doesn't answer, so I go to the window instead and try to communicate with her through that. It's hard to see out in the darkness, but I can make out the shape of my wife standing on the lawn, a few yards away from the cabin. But I can't quite see her facial expression, though I can predict what it is. She'll either be angry or sad. Maybe a combination of both. She'll also have the key in her hand, the key that I need her to put back in the lock on this door so that we can get out of here.

'Grace! Come on! Open this door!'

Another desperate plea goes unanswered before I notice a light has just been switched on in here. Turning around, I see Kamilla standing by the desk, one arm awkwardly but strategically covering her bare chest, while the other covers her groin. The lamp on my desk is glowing, offering a little light but not much because I never needed it to be particularly bright considering I did all of my work at my desk during daylight hours. But it's better than nothing and certainly better than being in complete darkness.

Then Kamilla asks me a question.

'What the hell is your wife doing here?'

'I don't know! She was supposed to be staying in a hotel!'

'Well, guess what? She isn't!'

Kamilla looks panicked, as she has every right to be, because who would want to be trapped in the home of the wife whose husband you've been sleeping with?

'Look, everything will be okay. I'll talk to her.'

'How? She's locked us in!'

'She'll let us out.'

'Will she?'

'Yes, she's just in shock. She needs to calm down.'

The thought of what must have gone through my wife's mind when she walked in here and saw us is enough to make me feel disgusting, not to mention embarrassed, but I can't dwell on that at the moment. I need to focus on improving the situation before it gets any worse.

'We can't even get dressed! All our clothes are in the house!' Kamilla laments, and she is right. We have nothing to wear in here because we were so consumed by our passion that we came into the garden without a single stitch of clothing between us.

The fact that I can't cover my dignity means I'm going to have to try and calm my wife down while naked, which feels like it's making an impossible task even harder. If this was a movie, I'd be laughing at my character right about now. But this is real life, my life, and it's quickly becoming more of a tragedy than a comedy.

I have no choice. All I can do is put one hand over my private parts and the other hand to the window as I knock against the glass and try to get Grace to answer me.

'I'm sorry! I really am. Just let me out so we can talk!'

I can still see the shape of my wife out there on the lawn through the pale moonlight, but she's not moving, and her stillness is becoming disconcerting. The quietness out there is just as disturbing. At least if she was screaming at me and hurling abuse then I would know exactly where I stand with her. But I'm getting nothing back from her at the moment.

Nothing but the locked door in between us.

I try the door again, squeezing the handle and twisting it as hard as I can, as well as pulling on it too, for good measure. But I don't succeed in getting the door open, which should always be the case considering that it's locked. After all, I paid the builder good money to make sure this place was secure from any potential intruders and thieves. It's just a shame that security is now the thing keeping me trapped inside here.

What if Grace doesn't let us out?

What if she wants to torment us for a little while?

Knowing what I know about the cabin and its construction, it isn't the easiest place to get out of.

Despite my desperation to open this door, my companion in the cabin doesn't seem quite as eager to be set free.

‘What’s she going to do to me?’ Kamilla ponders, looking very afraid. ‘Would she get violent? Will she attack me?’

‘No, of course not.’

‘But she must hate me. I’d hate me too if I’d found my husband having sex with another woman!’

‘She’s not going to get violent. She’s just upset. We just need to get this door open so you can go home, and then I’ll talk to her.’

‘How am I supposed to go home? I have to get all my clothes from your house! Is she just going to stand by and watch me pick them all up? Or will she help me? Pass me my bra while I compliment her on the wallpaper in the living room? This is ridiculous!’

Kamilla is right. This is ridiculous. But what does she want me to do about it? It’s almost as if she is blaming me for what’s happened, but I didn’t plan on getting caught any more than she did.

‘Just stay calm. Everything will be okay,’ I say, but it’s extremely unconvincing because the longer we’re stuck in here, the less sure I am that everything will be.

‘Don’t you have a spare key or something?’ Kamilla asks, looking around at my desk and the shelf above it.

‘Yes, but it’s under the plant pot over there, which isn’t much use to us here!’

‘What about the window? Can’t you open it?’

‘It can’t be opened. It’s more secure that way.’

‘So what do we have to do to get out? Smash the glass?’

I shake my head because that's not even an option.

'It's toughened. Triple glazed so nobody could break in.'

'What? Why have you made it so secure?'

'Because I keep important work documents in here! I can't have them being stolen, can I?'

'It's a bit of boring paperwork! You didn't need to build Fort Knox!'

Kamilla might have a point, but what can I say? We had the budget to make this place burglar-proof when we built it, and I went for it. Little did I know I'd end up being the one that the toughened doors and windows frustrated the most.

'But how are we going to get out if she doesn't unlock the door?' Kamilla asks me, her once low, sexy voice now high-pitched and whiney.

'I don't know. I never thought I'd get locked in here, did I?'

Arguing with each other isn't going to help us, so I turn back to the window and hope to converse with Grace instead. But when I look out, I can't see her anywhere.

She's gone.

'Grace? Grace!'

I bang on the window but despite that, she doesn't appear again. Where is she? Has she gone back inside the house? What the hell is she playing at? She can't keep us locked in here all night.

Then I remember it. The famous old saying. It's one that's as old as time, but it's also one that my late father used to use a lot whenever my mum would tell him off for doing something he shouldn't have done, which was usually him coming in late from the pub or not helping out around the house when he had promised he would.

"Hell hath no fury like a woman scorned."

I know what it means. It's a saying to show that there is no anger as strong as that of a woman who has been romantically betrayed. But that's what I've done to Grace. I've betrayed her, and now she is a scorned woman, capable of anything.

Like keeping her husband and his mistress under lock and key for as long as she sees fit.

'Oh God,' I say to myself when I think about how stubborn my wife can be over even the smallest of things. Now she has something to really be stubborn over.

This is bad. Really, really bad.

Grace has been hurt. But she also has all the power.

What happens next is entirely up to her.

But what will it be?

5

GRACE

I'm gripping the key in my hand so tightly that it's starting to hurt me. But I can't help it. My anger is such that even the discomfort of the metal digging into my skin is not enough to make me stop squeezing. Nor is it going to let me even consider putting the key back in that lock and releasing the two people trapped inside the cabin.

They deserve this.

They have brought this on themselves.

Whatever happens next is entirely justified.

Whether I actually believe that or not is beside the point. This key and what I have used it to do so far is not only a symbol of my heartache, but it's also a symbol of my future. Whatever I decide to do with it next, be it good or bad, carries consequences. And they are consequences that all three of us here in this back garden tonight will have to live with.

I'm still standing on the grass staring at the two shapes in the cabin window, shapes that are not moving in the same way. The female form is much more mobile, all flailing arms as she bangs on the window, while the male form is more still, more considerate.

Or perhaps just more resigned to his fate.

I wonder if Dominic has told his lover yet about how it isn't possible for them to break out of that cabin. I know just how impossible it is because Dominic spent a lot of time telling me about how he was making it super-secure so that nobody could ever break in. In all that time during the development stage of this cabin, I don't think he ever considered that it wasn't somebody breaking in that should be the concern but somebody breaking out.

Of course, I didn't consider it either because I had never planned on locking anybody inside the cabin, let alone the man I married. But thanks to how much he stressed this structure had to be impenetrable to anybody who didn't have the access key, we now find ourselves in this interesting predicament.

His mistress, the woman I hate above all others in this world now, is still banging on the windows, so either she doesn't know that she is wasting her time yet, or she is just choosing to ignore Dominic and what he might have told her about the reinforced glass. How I wish she had chosen to ignore my husband full stop because if she had done that then we could have avoided this mess.

How did these two meet? That's what I want to know. What set of circumstances brought them together? I'm intrigued, not that it really matters. Did they bump into each other in a coffee shop? Did she drop something, and he helped her pick it up, behaving like a true gentleman with no ulterior motive? Perhaps they found themselves standing beside one another in a queue, and she asked him for the time before noting his nice watch and figuring she might try and snare herself a naïve sugar daddy to have some fun with. Or did he strike up the first conversation, awkwardly trying not to look at her impressive cleavage as he mumbled something about the weather, while wondering if there was any chance a woman like her might fancy a guy like him?

There are a million ways they could have met, and however it occurred, it was bad luck for me. But I bet they considered it good luck on their part and possibly even blissful destiny once they were rolling around on top of each other behind my back. But considering what has just happened, they surely have to consider the fact that their paths crossing was nothing but utter misfortune now. However they met, they also both had to have known that taking things as far as they did was wrong.

She knew she was getting involved with a married man, right? Or did he hide the fact he was involved with somebody else from her? Did he remove his wedding ring when he first saw her or slip it off discreetly during their initial exchange? Did she even know about me? Is she almost as shocked as I am?

No, she must have known Dominic had a wife. She couldn't have missed all the wedding photos on the wall in the house. Well, not unless she was too carried away taking her clothes off and getting my man to do the same, and considering the size of the debris field that their clothes made around my house, that is a possibility.

But who knows? Not me. My imagination and paranoia are running so wild now that I'm considering all sorts of horrible things about the man I married. Like what if he pretended to her that I had died? Is that it? Did he play the widow card to get some sympathy?

Surely not. Dominic wouldn't be capable of such a despicable thing, would he? I don't know; he's clearly capable of all sorts.

He's clearly not the man I thought he was.

As I continue to stand and watch the figures in the cabin window try to get my attention, I hope that the woman locked inside did know exactly what she was getting herself into when she decided to sleep with Dominic. That way, I don't have to feel one iota of sympathy for her, just like I feel none for my husband, and that makes it a hell of a lot easier to keep them both under lock and key.

Deciding that I will increase the misery of the pair a little more, I turn and walk away from the cabin, nonchalantly strolling across the grass and back to the house as if I don't have a care in the world. I hope they'll be able to see me and my casual stride for as long as possible, but the reality is that it's dark out here, and I'm probably out of sight long before I make it back to the kitchen door and re-enter my home.

My home. The one littered with the discarded clothing of the woman who has been sleeping with my man. All her things are still littering my space.

It's time to do something about that.

I get to work, moving around the house and picking her things up quickly. The heels. The blouse. *The skirt that makes me sick.* All of the things that she took off so happily are now the things I am collecting so sadly.

I take care to make sure I've got everything, not wanting to miss something and see it later where it could upset me all over again. But it takes a while to be certain and I even get down on my hands and knees and check under the sofas to be sure that there aren't any lacey garments residing under there. Thankfully, there are not and once I'm satisfied that I have all of her things, I go back out to the garden and dump them all in the middle of the lawn. Then I return to the house and collect my husband's clothes, but I don't just limit myself to the few items he has lying around on the floor downstairs. Oh no, that would be wasteful. I make sure to go upstairs too, to our bedroom, the one we have slept in so many times together, and once there, I start to empty out the wardrobe and cupboards that belong to him.

His shirts. His socks. His stupid suits. Everything I can get my hands on comes out of the place it belongs and ends up in one big pile in the middle of the bed. Then I wrap my arms around it all and carry the clothes as best I can downstairs until I deposit them beside *her things* on the cold, slightly damp grass.

I go back and forth from the house over the next twenty minutes, picking up more things that belong to Dominic and giving them a new home outside. But I've graduated from clothes now and have moved on to other things, possibly more personal to him, or at least I hope so. Like his books, including his favourite, *The Lord Of The Rings,* a special edition hardback book that he was gifted by his grandparents and one that he has thumbed through several times over the years. I also target his sports memorabilia, including the signed photo of his favourite football player in action that he bid for and won in a charity auction at a works event a couple of years ago. And of course, I have to go for his record collection, the assortment of music that he has accrued over his lifetime and features all sorts of songs and artists that remind him of some of the happiest moments of his youth.

Everything he owns is now lying on the grass, getting dirty, just like he was lying on the ground of that cabin not so long ago getting dirty with a woman he had no right to be getting involved with.

With the pile at my feet high and wide, I look back to the cabin window to see if the people on the other side of the glass have noticed what I have been doing. The fact I can see two still shapes staring back at me confirms that they have been watching, and that makes me smile.

They have the best seats in the house.

Two tickets to the show that I'm about to put on for them.

And what a show it is going to be.

6

DOMINIC

'What is she doing with all our things?' Kamilla keeps asking me, and while I know I should try and answer her, all I can keep thinking about is how it isn't actually all *our* things.

It's all *my things*.

All she has out there are a few items of clothing, which are things that can easily be replaced. But from what I can see, almost everything I own is now sitting in a big pile in the middle of the back garden, and what's there will not be so easy to get back.

All my clothes, including some of the suits that definitely should not be lying on damp grass. My books, a collection that is bound to include my favourite and the one story I was planning on re-reading at the end of the year. My music collection - records that remind me of simpler times and records that I had planned on storing in my cabin and really wish I had moved in here already because it seems they would be safer in here than out there right now. And even my prized signed sports photo that I successfully bid for in an auction, the photo that was going to be hung on a wall in this cabin, but I couldn't find any nails in the garage last week, so I had put that off too. *Damn it.*

All things that I either need or cherish, symbols of my personality and interests, piled on top of each other as if they were worth nothing more than a load of scrap metal in a junkyard. And all put there by my wife, a woman I have severely scorned and now somebody who is clearly looking to take revenge on me.

So what's her move here? Is this her way of telling me that she's kicking me out? By emptying the house of all my things? I guess so. Well, okay, Grace, you have made your point. You want me to leave and take my things with me so that you can have some time and space to think. So be it. While I'd rather try and make things better immediately, I understand that. Forgiving me isn't going to be a quick process. If I have to live elsewhere for a short while then I'll find somewhere. I'll get a room in a cheap hotel and keep trying to make amends from there until you let me and all my possessions back in our house where we belong.

But that is still up for debate at the moment because until I get out of here, I can't do much of anything other than try desperately to cover my most intimate parts while peering through the window and wondering when you're going to unlock this door.

'I knew we should have just kept it to hotel rooms,' Kamilla says, referring to where the two of us could have limited our illicit rendezvous.

'Me too. But you got bored of those and told me you wanted to do it at my place,' I remind her, not mentioning that I hadn't needed much persuading after the fact. That was because I had been so confident that I could keep all of this a secret. Keep both plates spinning simultaneously. Have my mistress here while my wife was elsewhere. *Have my cake and eat it.* But what right did I have to think this would go so smoothly? There's a reason not everyone has an affair, and even fewer people get away with it.

Because it's not easy.

I can still see my things out there on the grass, but I can't see Grace, so I guess she's gone back into the house. Is she getting more things of mine? What else could be left? I wonder if she would be so crazed as to drive my car around the back and park it on top of everything, making a very big statement, but I doubt she'll do something as dramatic as that, or at least I hope not. She might reverse the car up to the pile though, so it's easier to throw all my stuff into the back of it before she makes me drive it all out of here.

Kamilla's trying the door again, but I'll leave her to figure out that it's still as much of a waste of time as it was the last time she tried it. While she's busy with that, I'm busy thinking ahead several weeks and months to hopefully figure out how long it will take me to be back in my wife's good graces. By my birthday in October? Christmas? The New Year? Or will this run into the early months of next year, through the deepest, darkest part of winter.

The winter of my extreme discontent.

I'm aware that the longer it takes for me to get Grace to forgive me, the less chance I have of it happening at all, in the long run. That's because the more time she lives without me, the more she might realise that she won't die if I'm not around every day. She might realise that she can exist without me, and where does that leave me then? In a poxy motel eating takeaway pizza and trying to figure out how to meet other desperate and lonely middle-aged people just like me.

I'm also aware that the more time Grace has to think about this, the more opportunity for her to share her plight with others and get their opinion on things. Friends, colleagues, a wise old woman at a bus stop. I'm sure they'd all be more than happy to offer their two cents about me and what I've done.

"A leopard doesn't change its spots."

"Once a cheat, always a cheat."

"Screw him. There's plenty more fish in the sea."

I imagine them all saying that and more. But they still don't know what's happened. Not yet. Only Grace knows what I've done, so what if I could just get out of here and talk to her and make it so that she never has to tell anybody else what happened here? This could all blow over if so and that prospect is highly appealing.

I'll do anything to make it so. Counselling. Therapy. Sleeping in the spare bedroom for six months. Whatever it takes. I just need a chance.

To explain.

To make it right.

To get out of this damn cabin.

I bang on the window again while Kamilla keeps trying the door, but in all that time, Grace doesn't reappear outside. The longer this goes on, the more this place that I loved so much is quickly feeling like a prison from which I'll never escape, and I bet my wife finds it hilarious that I'm being tormented by something I fought so hard to have built. Or at least she would find it hilarious if she probably wasn't in the house crying her eyes out.

Is that what she's doing? Wailing and sobbing and asking God why he would let such a horrible thing happen to her? Or is she having a strong drink while texting her boss to say that she won't be in tomorrow but that she has the biggest piece of news that they're likely to hear this decade?

'I don't know what to do,' I admit, as much to myself as to the naked woman beside me as I sit down on my office chair and feel the cold leather of the seat against my pale, exposed skin. I've never felt so helpless in all my life. I'm as naked as the day as I was born, and I feel as useless as it too.

I stare down at my wriggling toes for a few moments until I hear Kamilla finally stop trying to open the door. When I look up at her, I see the way she is staring at me, and she has a look in her eyes that I've never seen her possess around me before.

No longer is she looking at me like I'm the attractive older man who could make all her fantasies come true. Now, she is looking at me for what I feared I was before I met her - a pathetic, middle-aged loser way past his prime and afraid that his best days are behind him.

She sees me for who I really am, and if I didn't know it before, I know it now.

I've thrown away the love of a great woman for the love of a woman who always would have got bored of me in the end.

‘Do something,’ Kamilla tells me, and I can sense her disdain at me growing by the second. It’s as if she is wondering what she ever saw in me at the exact same time my wife is doing the same thing outside.

‘I don’t know what to do,’ I reply meekly.

Kamilla shakes her head before looking around, and I watch her hopelessly, wishing for her to find something that could help us but knowing that she can’t.

Her eyes land on the plug socket behind me and the cables that extend out from it, and that gives her an idea.

‘Do you have internet in here?’

‘Yeah, why?’

‘We could contact somebody. Where’s your laptop?’

It seems a shame to extinguish the hope in Kamilla’s eyes no sooner than it has appeared, but that’s what I have to do.

‘In the house. Or at least it was. It’s probably on that pile in the garden now.’

‘For God’s sake, Dom! Why didn’t you just leave it in here? We could have emailed somebody from it!’

‘I always took it back into the house in case someone broke into the cabin.’

‘But nobody can break in! You’ve made this place impenetrable, inside and out!’

‘I know but-’

‘-but what?’

‘I was always paranoid, so I took the laptop to the house at the end of the day.’

'Paranoid? The only thing you should have been paranoid about is that wacko out there. Seriously, who have you married? Do you even know her?'

'What? Of course I do! And she isn't a wacko. Don't call her that.'

'She's not a wacko, is she not?' Kamilla asks as she looks out of the window, and there's something about her accusatory tone of voice that makes me sense dread.

'No,' I mumble, nervous and upset.

'Ok then, 'Kamilla says with a shake of the head. 'Then please explain to me why she is about to set fire to all of our things?'

I leap out of the chair and rush to the window after hearing that, and as I look out, I'm just in time to see the first shoots of flames spreading across the pile of our belongings.

Kamilla's clothes and everything I own.

All about to go up in smoke.

And my wife's face lit up as she stands over the growing bonfire and smiles.

7

GRACE

What is it about fire that makes it so fantastical to watch? What is it that draws people to a raging inferno, causing them to stop and stare?

The danger? The destruction? The death that can occur from its fiery depths?

Kids and adults alike struggle to divert their eyes from flames, whether it's while sitting around a campfire or gathering around a bonfire on November 5th. There is no denying there is something mesmerising about fire. The way the oranges, reds and yellows lick at each other as they devour anything they come into contact with.

At the moment, these particular flames are devouring everything from my husband's books to his hussy's undergarments, and I am taking pleasure from watching it all burn. I am deriving particular pleasure from witnessing her bra turning to ashes. No longer is it white and pure, but now it is as black and sullied as the heart of the woman who once wore it.

But I've made sure that this isn't a show for just one to enjoy. The couple in the cabin will be able to see my triumphant display of revenge, and as I notice them watching from the window, I hope they are burning on their insides just as much as their things are burning on the outside.

They can't hate me for this, surely. What did they expect me to do? Put their clothes into a neat pile and hand them over with compliments from the woman whose house they just explored each other's bodies in?

This isn't some hotel offering five-star service and seeking a five-star review.

This is a marital home, a sacred space.

But now it's just a place that smells of burning.

I think about my neighbours, Frank and Maggie, and wonder what they will think if and when they smell the smoke. They'll know it's far too late in the evening for a barbecue, so they might venture out of their house to come and check if everything is okay next door. They will if they think there might be something wrong, and how can there not be when a fire has taken hold in the middle of the night?

But maybe they're already asleep, and if so, they might not have any inkling of the pyromaniacal pleasure occurring so close to them. That will be good because I don't really want to have to explain to Frank or Maggie why I'm burning things so late at night.

I don't want to have to explain that I'm burning everything my man ever bought.

But it's not everything, is it? There is still something here that he bought that is not alight. Something he cherishes as much as everything in this fiery pile, if not more.

The cabin.

What if I was to set fire to that?

The thought is as fleeting as some of the embers that rise up from the flames and burn up in the sky because while it would be wonderful to see the panic on the couple's faces as they realised that I was preparing to burn them alive, I know such a thing is ultra-extreme, even for a scorned woman like me.

I could and would love to set fire to that cabin but not with them in it. But to burn that hideous structure to the ground without them inside it would mean letting them out, and I'm not ready to do that yet.

I can see them both watching the fire from the cabin and of course they are because a fire demands attention, doesn't it? Maybe that's what I needed to do before this happened. Be more like fire. Demand the attention of my husband and once I have it, keep it. As it is, I let his attention be captured by somebody else, and while I can win it back with a series of stunts like locking the door and starting a fire, I know it's probably all only temporary.

Unless I can keep coming up with ways to make Dominic watch me.

The fire is strong enough to do what I need it to do, and I have no doubt that it will burn everything in this pile if I leave it long enough, but I want more attention, and that means I need a bigger blaze. A quick visit to the kitchen sees me remove a bottle of cooking oil from the cupboard, and when I go back to the flaming pile, I squirt several torrents of the stuff onto it, making the fire hiss, spit and most importantly, grow.

I can feel the heat on my face as I get a little too close to the blaze, but I stand there for a moment or two longer, like a child on Bonfire Night, ignoring the warnings from their parents to step back because for that one brief moment, they have never felt more alive in their little lives.

I certainly feel alive now as I make the fire grow bigger and bigger, and it's only the fear that I might end up setting the whole garden alight that eventually snaps me out of my daydream and makes me think about putting this inferno out.

Dragging myself away from the tantalising flames, I grab the mop bucket from under the kitchen sink and fill it under the tap before returning to the garden and slowly pouring cold water onto the fire, dousing the incinerated pile while careful not to cause any splashback. I might have acted rashly several times tonight, from choosing to come home early to locking the cabin door and starting a fire, but now I'm acting rationally as I extinguish the fire sensibly. It's going out almost as quickly as it started, and I'm glad about that because it's late now, I'm very tired, and it's not time for making stupid mistakes.

I note the charred remains of the books as well as the cracked frame of the sports picture that will now never hang on the wall of the cabin to be shown off to friends by its proud owner. I also see the last remnants of that woman's bra, and as I hoped, it is now nothing but pure black.

Eventually, the fire is no more, fading feebly like a dying mammal that knew its fate but resisted until the bitter end anyway because that's what its survival instincts insist it does. But death comes for everything in the end, so it eventually goes out, and when it does, the garden is plunged back into darkness again.

I can no longer see the faces in the cabin.

And I guess they can no longer see me.

I change that by approaching the window and getting close enough to see the naked forms on the other side of it. How I bet they long for a little warmth on their skin from a fire like that one. They must be getting cold in there. The temperature always drops at night, and it's certainly dropped for me now that I'm no longer being warmed by the flames.

I know there's a heater in the cabin. It was only sensible that Dominic installed such a thing if he wanted to work in there all year round. But I also know that the only way it works is by being connected to the main electricity supply from the house, and disrupting that supply would render that heater utterly useless, which is kind of how I felt when I arrived home and found the pair together.

Shall I disconnect that power supply now? Leave them devoid of electricity?

No, or at least not yet, anyway. I'll allow them the option of warmth for the time being. No need to force them to seek each other's body heat yet.

They've already had enough of that.

Barring the odd snap or crackle from the smouldering pile behind me, all is quiet in this garden. Surprisingly quiet, actually, and that's because neither Dominic nor his floozy are calling out to me now. Nor are they banging on the window or rattling the door. They are just staring out at me, their sad, solemn little faces seeking sympathy.

Is this their new tactic? Make me feel sorry for them? Make it seem that we have all calmed down now and got our anger out of our systems, and that means it's time to unlock the cabin door and move on with our lives.

There's just one problem with that and it's that I'm not ready to move on.

I am ready to do something else though.

I'm ready to communicate.

Slowly raising my right hand towards the window, I hold my closed fist in front of me, turning the knuckles towards them so that they can get a good look at it. Then I ever so slowly raise the middle finger of that hand until it is pointing straight up in the air.

Yes, I'm swearing at them, and yes, it's a rude gesture. But it's important to do because it lets the pair know where they stand with me. No confusion now.

I still hate them.

Clearly.

Dominic's mistress doesn't like what I have just done and gets all angry again, but that only makes me repeat the same gesture with my other hand until I'm standing right in front of them, gesticulating like a schoolkid on the playground who has just learnt how to do something that teachers don't like. Only once I have got that out of my system do I lower my hands and mouth 'Goodnight' to the pair, before turning around and walking back to the house.

I hear them banging on the window as I enter the kitchen, but I can't hear them once I've locked it behind myself. Nor can I hear them once I'm upstairs in my bedroom, undressing for bed, or when I'm brushing my teeth in the bathroom and noticing how tired and pale my reflection looks.

I can't hear anything coming from the cabin in the garden, and more importantly, nobody else can hear anything either. With that the way it is, what is stopping me from keeping them in there for a long time? Nothing but my patience, I guess, and I've always had plenty of that. Now such a thing will be to that pair's detriment, just like it's been to other people's detriment in the past too.

Including my own.

8

GRACE

BEFORE MEETING DOMINIC

Anyone would assume a parent would be excited about the prospect of their daughter's upcoming birthday, particularly when it was a milestone one.

Turning thirty is a big deal, and I'm certainly looking forward to it.

But the same cannot be said of my mother, Diane.

I've always had an unorthodox relationship with the woman who gave birth to me. If I had to guess, I'd say that's because she was never completely sold on the idea of becoming a parent in the first place. At least that's where I assume I get it from because I'm not keen on having children either. It was my dad, Alan, who was more into parenthood, and I know this for a fact because I heard my two guardians arguing about it loudly many times when I was younger. I lost count of the number of times I'd be sitting upstairs in my bedroom listening to the pair of them arguing about a problem that seemed to have been made worse by my existence.

Money struggles. Tiredness. Lack of freedom. All exuberated by the little girl they had brought into the world together. I tried not to let it get me down, and to be fair, Mum and Dad both tried to pretend like I wasn't making things harder for them when I was in front of them, but I knew the truth because I overheard them when they didn't know I was eavesdropping. And the truth was that I put a strain on their relationship when I came on the scene.

But things between them didn't exactly get any easier once my parents' relationship was over.

Dad died when I was ten, meaning we're almost at the twenty-year anniversary of it being just me and Mum. A family of three became a family of two, but of course, a family with a parent missing is always lopsided, uneven, the imbalance felt by those left behind. Mum has never got over Dad's death, and while I haven't either, she's taken it far worse than me.

I only began to understand the depth of her loss as I got older and learnt all about love and relationships between a man and a woman and what it's like to have a soulmate. I didn't fully grasp it at the time, but I can see now that losing one is utterly devastating. Not that I would know from personal experience. I've not quite found my soulmate yet. There's been a few guys, but it's never lasted. But there's still time for me, or at least I hope there is.

But the big "three-o" is looming on the horizon, and I'm still single. That's okay. My biological clock never started ticking, so I'm not worried about it running out over the next decade. I'm happy enough as I am. But I would be happier if I found someone to share things with.

And I'd certainly be happier if my mum liked me.

I've been so patient with her over the years. I've always tried my best to improve our relationship and bring us closer together so that we could have the kind of mother-daughter relationship that others have and do the things they get to enjoy. Like going shopping together, sharing a coffee or a glass of wine together and maybe even going on holiday together. Those are all things that I would love to do with my mum, but as yet, we haven't done any of them since I reached adulthood. And that's why I'm not expecting her to want to make a big deal of my next birthday, even if it is a big one. A card and a smile are about the best I can hope for at this stage, but I think even that will be asking too much.

But I'll stay patient. I'll keep calling around to her house to visit her and make the effort, and I always will. I'll never give up on our relationship, even though she's made it clear that she's given up on it herself. And the reason for that is a simple one.

She blames me for Dad's death.

It's a horrible thing to put on a child, but that's the burden I must live with every day, knowing that my mother, the woman who should love me above all else in the world, despises me for the loss of her husband. I know that a lot of her anger and frustration towards me is tied up in never wanting me in the first place, so it's obvious to think that she believes her life would have turned out differently if she hadn't had me.

I'm sure she imagines an alternate universe, one where she stayed childless and, as a consequence, everything else was different. She would have had more money, more sleep, more time, and she probably imagines she'd still have her partner too. But who knows what could have happened if she hadn't had me. She might have struggled financially anyway, she still might not have had the energy or the time to do all the things she wanted to do in life, and there's certainly no saying that Dad would have lived if I hadn't come into the world. Bad things happen to people all the time, like accidents, illnesses, or he could simply have woken up one day and decided that he didn't want to be with her. It's unfair to blame everything on me. Yes, Mum's life might have been different if I hadn't been born, but then again, it might not. Only she can control her destiny. It's not right to put it all on me.

Then again, who am I kidding? We both know she is right. Things would have been so much better if I hadn't been born. It hurts that she knows it, but most of all, it hurts for me to know it myself.

Come on, Grace, pull yourself together. Don't think like this. Don't dwell on the past. What's done is done. It can't be changed. All you can do is look forward. Better times are ahead. Better times like birthdays.

It's seven days until my thirtieth, and I'd like to think that there's still time for Mum to surprise me. Invite me out for lunch or whisk me away for a spa treatment in a fancy hotel. Hell, at this point, I'd just take a phone call. That would be enough. It would certainly be preferable to going around to her place and knocking on her door only to find that she can't be bothered to answer.

But if Mum doesn't feel like celebrating my big day, then that's okay because I'll just find some other people to celebrate with. I have a few friends, mainly from work, but they'll do. I lost touch with all my childhood friends because I stopped going to school for a while after Dad died, and dealing with losing him made it hard for me to connect with people into my teenage years. But I'm not lonely, which is why I'm not particularly looking for a man. But if I was to find one, it wouldn't be the worst thing in the world, I suppose. I'd certainly not have to worry about who to spend my birthdays with then. A boyfriend would treat me on special occasions, that's for sure. Dinner and drinks. A nice piece of jewellery. Maybe even a romantic getaway in a European city. I can see why people like to be in a relationship. It creates more options. More things to do. More chances at having fun. Or at least it does until a child comes along and ruins everything, as in Mum's case.

Maybe I'll go to Mum's again today and have another go at trying to make things better between us. Another attempt at trying to show her that me being in her life isn't all bad news. Or maybe I'll just leave it and save myself the disappointment. I'll just carry on being alone while the days tick by until my birthday, and then I'll see who wants to come for a drink with me. One of the girls in the office will, I'm sure, and that's all I need.

Somebody to share something with. A drink. A night. A memory.

Little did I know it then, but my thirtieth birthday was going to be the night I met somebody I would end up sharing a lot with in my future.

The good times.

And the bad.

Somebody else's life was about to be changed by me coming into it.

And that somebody was eventually going to end up hating me too.

9

DOMINIC

The sight of my things burning in the fire that Grace started was galling for a number of reasons, but one of them was that I could have actually used some of that heat from the fire to keep myself warm in here. This cabin is getting chilly, and I'm going to have to try and turn the heater on because it's becoming increasingly apparent that Kamilla and I are going to be in here for a while. But I say try because I'm not sure if it's going to work when I flick the switch. I'm afraid that Grace might have disconnected the power and eliminated the electricity supply to this cabin, and if she has, that's when I'll really start to worry. Even the fact that the desk light is still on doesn't fill me with much confidence that the power won't be going out very shortly.

In the end, Kamilla decides to flick the switch on the heater herself.

'How long does it take to warm up?' she asks me as she stands shivering beside the heater that's only just been engaged, and I let out a sigh of relief when I hear the low rumble that tells me it is working.

'It's usually pretty quick. A couple of minutes at most,' I reply, still nervous about the prospect of my wife vindictively cutting our heat source. It's a wonderful relief when Kamilla exclaims that she can feel it hotting up, and as I join her to warm myself, I'm thankful Grace has so far declined the opportunity to make our miserable night even worse.

At least yet, anyway.

As Kamilla and I rub our hands together in front of the heater and take the chill out of our exposed skin, I find further comfort in the thought that the onset of the sunrise in a few hours' time will surely help bring this awful ordeal to a swift end. Grace just needs to rest and process things, but when she wakes up in the cold light of day and truly thinks about what she is doing, she will come to her senses quickly and unlock this door. How can she not? When she does, I can forgive her of it all, from the imprisonment to the bonfire, because I'll just be glad to be out in the sunlight. But for now, it's still dark, and that's why some more troubling thoughts are never far away, quickly able to swallow up the more optimistic ones and leave me staring out at the sky in search of that dim light on the horizon.

'There's no way she can be sleeping, right?' Kamilla asks me as she continues to warm herself by the heater. 'I mean, she'd have to be pretty messed up in the head to be able to close her eyes and drift off after what she's done tonight.'

'I'm sure she's awake,' I reply, hopeful but not certain. 'She's just cooling off. She'll be feeling better in the morning.'

'I thought she'd be feeling better after burning all our stuff. What's it been now? Three, four hours since she locked us in here?'

I'm not quite sure of the exact time because a watch is just one more thing I wasn't wearing when I came in here, but Kamilla's estimation sounds about right.

'We should try and get some rest ourselves,' I say, thinking practically because that's usually the best way to try and behave during a bad situation. 'You can lie down on the rug here next to the heater. It'll be more comfortable than the chair. Unless you want that?'

Kamilla hardly looks thrilled by the two options I have just given her, and that's to be expected because neither is exactly promising a good night's sleep. But it's the best we've got, and we both know it.

'Or we could have a drink,' I say, gesturing to the bottle of wine that I brought in here that currently sits on my desk, not because I'm feeling particularly thirsty or adventurous but because it at least gives us something to take the edge off our situation. But before I can pick up the bottle and take a swig, Kamilla raises a good point.

'What are we going to do about the bathroom situation?'

I don't have a good answer for that one other than to suggest both of us try and hold any ablutions until the morning, when we might be allowed out of here. But that's easier said than done, considering all the wine we drank earlier in the evening. With that in mind, I decide not to partake in any more.

'I have this,' I suggest, finding a cup on a shelf that I left in here the last time I was in the cabin.

'Great. That's perfect for me to use as a toilet,' Kamilla replies, shaking her head because it's anything but. 'You really know how to show a girl a good time.'

Kamilla doesn't take the cup from me, so I guess she isn't that desperate yet, nor do I need it, so I put it back on the desk. But it sits there in front of us, a constant reminder that it's our best bet for relieving ourselves at some point over the next few hours if we need to.

'Come on, let's try and rest,' I say, hoping that sleep might make this all a little more tolerable. 'We just need to get to the morning and then this will be over.'

'I'm not sure that it will be,' Kamilla replies, clearly not sharing in the confidence of my assessment.

'Why do you say that?'

'Think about it. What your wife has done here is illegal. I mean, what we have done is morally wrong, but what she has done to us is a criminal act. She's keeping us imprisoned against our will. She should be arrested for this, and she will be when I get out of here and tell the police what she did to us.'

'Woah, hang on, there's no need to bring the police into this.'

All of a sudden, my foolish act of adultery might not just be the concern of family and friends but the local law makers and peacekeepers. *No thanks.*

'But that's my point,' Kamilla goes on. 'Grace must know that I'd be tempted to report her to the authorities for this. So what if she keeps us in here so that can't happen?'

'Because she can't just make us both disappear without an explanation, can she? I'm her husband. People would ask questions about me if I just disappeared. She has to let me out.'

'Okay, so she has to let you out. But what about me? Nobody knows I was here tonight.'

'I do.'

'But will you take my side over hers?'

'Of course!'

'Really? Or will you just do anything to get your wife back?'

'I'll do the right thing by both of you.'

'What the hell does that mean?'

'It means I'm in a very awkward situation here, if you hadn't noticed, and I'm going to have to be very careful moving forward. Of course I want to get you out of here so you can go home, but I also have to try and manage my wife's emotions and not do anything that might anger her any more than she already is. And you bringing up the police isn't going to help matters, is it?'

'I'm sorry if being held against my will and having my clothes burned by a crazy woman is enough to make me want to go to the police!'

'Stop calling her crazy.'

'No, I won't because that's what she is! She is crazy! Crazy, crazy, crazy!'

The desk light suddenly goes off, along with the heater and anything else that might need an electricity supply to keep it going, and it's as if Grace has reacted to Kamilla and her angry rant. But is that it? Has my wife heard what has been said? It's doubtful if she's still in the house. Unless she isn't. Unless she came back out and has been eavesdropping on our conversation all this time from the other side of the cabin door.

‘Grace! Are you there?’ I call out as I rush to the door and put my hand on it as if touching it could help me bridge this gap.

But I get no response, and all is quiet until Kamilla proceeds to try and make things even worse for us by shouting and calling my wife all sorts of names all over again.

I plead with her to calm down and try and explain how this isn’t going to help us get out of here, but even while doing that, I’m starting to fear that my mistress is right. Grace is crazy. I mean, I gave her some allowance for catching us in the act. The locking of the door and even the burning of the clothes could have been done in haste. A crime of passion, as such. But this is going on for too long now, and cutting the power supply to the cabin is the last straw. This is going beyond just being a little bit of punishment for two people who have been up to something they shouldn’t have.

Now she has killed the heater, this is starting to get dangerous.

It is starting to get life-threatening.

No wonder Kamilla is talking about the police. They would certainly be interested in hearing about what Grace has been up to here tonight. But they can’t hear about it because it’s not over yet, and there’s no saying when it will be.

How will this end?

I have no idea.

I only know how it all began.

10

DOMINIC

THE MEETING

I hadn't been planning to go out this evening. I was just going to finish work, go home, get some food and have an early night. But then one of my colleagues quite rightly reminded me that I was thirty, not ninety, so I should put less emphasis on my beauty sleep and more emphasis on having a good time while I'm still young. Or at least that's the excuse I'm using as I stand by this bar in a busy venue in the town centre.

In truth, I've never needed much persuading to abandon a night of rest and recuperation in favour of partying with pals, so it's hardly a surprise to myself or anyone who knows me that I'm out late now, drinking far more than I should on a worknight, having long ago abandoned the thought of my bed and what benefits eight solid hours of sleep could do for me tomorrow.

But as I stand here and order another drink while several of my work colleagues chat loudly around me, I'm aware that there is another reason why I wasn't quick to say no to the offer of company tonight. It's because if I hadn't then I'd be by myself now, back at my 'bachelor pad', the place I've been living by myself ever since my last relationship ended two years ago and a place where I've spent far too many nights wondering if I'll ever find the right woman and settle down.

I'm not feeling too sorry for myself because despite my non-existent love life of late, everything else is in order. I have a good job, good health and good friends. I know I'm lucky to have those things, and I don't take them for granted. But I am missing that special someone to come along and really take my life to the next level. Romance. Passion. Love. I won't admit it to my mates because they would call me soft and soppy, but the truth is, I'd like nothing more than to meet a woman who could give me all of those things, and that's why I've been keeping an eye out this evening for anybody in this bar who could potentially be my future wife.

Alas, I've had little luck so far, although that might be mainly down to the reason I haven't spoken to any members of the opposite sex since I've been here. But the night is still young. It's only nine, and one more drink should see me possess enough Dutch courage to approach at least one of the lovely ladies in this place.

As it turns out, I spend most of the next hour chatting to one of my work friends about how it would be great if we had a more generous annual leave allowance, rather than putting in any real effort to find love in here. Now it's getting late, time is running out, and I'm hardly helping my chances of ending my status as a singleton.

It's looking very much like I'll be going home alone.

Again.

By the time I leave the bar, my mood is in the gutter, but surprisingly, that's where I find somebody who would very quickly go on to change the course of my life forever, not that I was to know it at the time. There's a woman sitting by herself on the edge of the pavement outside the bar. She's wearing a black dress, heels and looks very much like she came out to have a good time this evening, just like me. But also like me, it doesn't look like she found it because despite the noise from the bar behind us and the engines of the passing cars on the street ahead, I can hear the sound of something very sobering.

This woman is crying.

Trying to be more of a gentleman than any kind of lothario, I approach the woman to check on her wellbeing.

'Are you okay?' I ask her as I stand awkwardly beside her, looming over her a little, but I have no other choice considering that she's sat on the ground.

The woman looks up at me with tears in her eyes and mascara running down her cheeks, and if there's a sorrier sight in the world than this right now, I'd be surprised. But she makes no attempt to cover up her distress, and if anything, she only starts to get more upset by my question.

'I'm sorry. I just wanted to see if there was anything I could do to help,' I say, wondering what could have happened to cause this poor person to have such a bad night. Has she had an argument with her boyfriend? Has she been stood up? Or has she just had too much to drink and got overly emotional about something silly? I don't know, but I'd sure like to. I'd like to help her if I can, and I repeat that desire to her after she fails to answer me the first time.

'I'm okay,' she eventually tells me, but it's possibly the most incorrect use of that statement by a person ever because she is still sobbing, and that mascara is still running down her cheeks.

'Well, if you're not going to tell me what's wrong, I'm just going to have to sit down here beside you and keep you company with my bad conversational skills until you do.'

I sit down on the edge of the pavement next to her then, not willing to leave her out here by herself in this state because not only is it unsafe, but I know I wouldn't be doing the right thing by just walking away from somebody who clearly needs a shoulder to cry on.

'You don't have to be nice to me,' she tells me, making some attempt at wiping her tears away, but it only causes her mascara to smudge further, and despite her bedraggled appearance, the worse she looks, the more I find her endearing. She's certainly different to all the other women out here tonight with their pristine make-up and without a single hair out of place on their heads. This woman is more real, more natural. *More honest.* Life isn't perfect, and instead of everybody here pretending that it is, it seems I've found somebody who is willing to admit the truth. The truth that despite the brave face we put on every day, we all need somebody, but we can't always find them.

'You're right. I don't have to be nice to you,' I say with a smile. 'But how else am I going to get you to buy me a drink in that bar unless I try and chat you up a little bit first?'

That gets a laugh out of the woman, and for the first time since I laid eyes on her, I see that she has a beautiful smile. Now it becomes my goal to try and make that smile become more permanent and help her forget about her troubles, whatever they may be, and I do so by telling her all about my night or rather, how it's not gone quite as planned for me either.

'I'm supposed to be in bed right now, so I'm fresh for work tomorrow. But instead, I've spent the last few hours drinking too much beer and making some very ill-advised moves on the dancefloor, and that's why, despite my best efforts, I am still single. And now I'll have to try and cover up my hangover from my boss tomorrow, which won't be easy because I get the world's worst hangovers, and if you think I am exaggerating about that then you are welcome to come and visit me at my office in the morning and see for yourself. I'll be the one with my head down on my desk at 9am surrounded by fizzy drinks, sugary snacks and a deep sense of regret.'

I get another laugh from the woman, and she has definitely stopped crying now, so I take that as a good point to introduce myself and hopefully coax her name out of her.

'I'm Dominic,' I say as I hold my hand out towards her. 'And you are?'

'Grace.'

‘It’s nice to meet you, Grace. I have to say, you might be the first person I’ve met sitting on the side of a road outside a bar.’

‘Really? I bet you meet girls like this all the time.’

I take her teasing me as a good sign and laugh before I gently broach the subject of her distress once again. And this time, she is more receptive to letting me know what’s wrong.

‘It’s my birthday today,’ Grace tells me, which doesn’t sound like an obvious problem to me.

‘Happy birthday!’

‘No, it’s not.’

‘Why, what’s happened?’

‘I’ll give you a clue. I’ve been out since seven o’clock; it’s now nearly eleven, and you’re the first person who has spoken to me all night.’

‘What do you mean?’

‘I mean I’ve spent my birthday night alone. Nobody wanted to celebrate with me. Not my work colleagues. Not the few friends I have who I asked to meet for a drink. And not even my mum. She didn’t even answer the door to me when I went around to see her today.’

I really don’t know what to say to all of that except that it sounds terrible. I can’t imagine my family and friends treating me with such indifference on my birthday. But it certainly explains why Grace is so upset.

‘I’m so sorry. That sounds awful. But I’m here, so how about I buy you a birthday drink? I mean, I know

I'm just some stranger but aren't we all until we get to know each other?'

'You'd do that for me?'

Grace looks genuinely surprised that somebody would be nice to her, which only makes me want to cheer her up even more.

'Are you kidding? Of course! Come on, let's go inside and have a look at that cocktail menu.'

'But I thought you had work tomorrow?'

'I do, but some things are more important than that, and celebrating a birthday is one of them.'

'But you don't even know me.'

'Yes, I do. I know that your name is Grace. I know that you have a very pretty smile. And I also know that you have just turned twenty-one, not that you look a day over twenty.'

Grace bursts out laughing then, which was my intention with that joke about her age.

'Don't be silly, you know I'm not twenty-one.'

'Maybe not, but a man can't ask a woman her age, can he?'

'I don't mind telling you. I'm thirty today.'

The fact her birthday is a big milestone only makes what she has been through today even more tragic, but while there is still an hour left of the day, there is time for me to turn this around for her. I'm not thinking of trying to sleep with her later or maybe make her my girlfriend one day, and I'm certainly not thinking about going down on one knee in the future and popping the question to her once I'm overcome with love and happiness around her. All I am thinking about doing at that moment in time is cheering her up.

And amazingly, it works. Grace keeps smiling for the rest of the night as we drink, dance and eventually, kiss.

And that was how it all started.

The beginning of our romance.

The start of our relationship.

There was no way back then that I was to know how it would end.

11

GRACE

I know that disconnecting the power to the cabin was a harsh move, but after trying and failing to get to sleep, it was the only thing I could think to do to give myself a little bit of happiness. I'd spent too long lying in bed thinking about Dominic and that woman at the bottom of the garden and wondering if the warmth from the heater in the cabin was making things a little too comfortable for them. Or maybe it was the thought that both of them were in there, naked and hot, that drove me to cut the power and make things a little less warm in there.

Okay, so cooling things down might not be the best way of keeping them apart because they could very well be snuggling up together to get some of each other's body heat now, but I'd rather them be shivering than sweating. And I know for a fact that the male body, or at least certain parts of it, doesn't tend to do as well in the cold compared to the warmth.

The thought of Dominic in the cabin, covering up his modesty as he shivers and shakes, is an amusing one, but the fun of it started to wear off as the night wore on, and I found it impossible to get some rest. I tried everything from a cup of chamomile tea to listening to an app that plays soothing songs, but none of it worked. Sleep is impossible, and maybe it will be for as long as I have that couple locked away.

The dead of night is never a good time to do some soul searching because everything seems so bleak when the sky is dark, and the streets are quiet. Better to do that kind of thing in the day when life doesn't seem so scary. *Or quiet.* The silence in this house is almost deafening, and that's why I decide to get up and make a little bit of noise, opting to have a shower and distract myself with the torrents of hot water blasting over my ears, for a few minutes at least.

This is a shower that Dominic and I have made love in in the past, although not for many years now. That's more my fault than his because he still suggested it on occasion, but I always turned him down, laughing off the idea of it as if we were too old to even entertain such a thing. But are we? Or did I just stop learning how to have fun somewhere along the way?

'No,' I say out loud to myself as the hot water continues to run over my skin and disappear down the plughole by my feet. This is not my fault. My brain might want to suggest all sorts of ways in which I drove my husband into the arms of somebody else but me not wanting to have sex with him in the shower is not one of them. It's not unreasonable for me to want to keep things to the bedroom. And it's not unreasonable for me to want my husband to keep it in his trousers when I'm not around.

I wonder if he's told his other woman how she's more adventurous than me. Possibly even used it as an excuse. *"My wife used to be so much fun, but she tricked me. She changed, and now I'm forced to get my fun elsewhere. If only she let me do what I want, then this wouldn't have happened. Therefore, it can't be my fault, can it?"*

I wouldn't put it past him to say those things now I know what else he is capable of doing.

It feels good to have a wash, although there are some things that soap cannot scrub away, and the thought that I'm holding two people against their will is one of them. I bet Dominic and that woman would love a shower right now. They'd also love some fresh clothes and a comfortable bed. But they aren't getting any of those things. The prisoners on Alcatraz weren't this deprived, but then again, those prisoners were only breaking the law. The couple in the cabin have broken something much worse, something that might never be repaired again. They've broken my heart as well as my ability to trust another human being. That's not legally a crime, but it should be. If there can be sentences given out for murder or armed robbery, then there should be a term of punishment assigned to relationship betrayals because those can be just as devastating as any act of physical violence that results in bloodshed.

I stay in the shower for far too long, not that the growing water bill is high on my list of concerns at present, before I eventually step out and wrap myself up in a warm towel. I change into a fresh pair of pyjamas and quickly dry my hair before making myself another cup of tea and consulting the clock on the kitchen wall.

04:05.

Dawn is still a couple of hours away. Should I go back to bed and have another go at getting some rest? No, I already know it's futile. Images of that woman with her hands all over my man are seared onto my brain and likely will be for some time yet. It's then that I regret burning everything I found here that belonged to her, not just her clothes but her handbag with her purse and phone in. Why was I so hasty? I could have learnt so much about her if I had only kept a cool head and taken the time to look. But anger overpowered all rational thought, and I burnt everything that woman possessed, no matter how helpful it might have been to me or how expensive it might have been for her.

But does it really matter what her name is? The details aren't important. The fact is she is another female form, a nameless figure who has come into my home and turned my life upside down. Finding out that she might be called Kathy, or Sue, or Sarah won't really make much difference to me at this point. And depending on how long I keep her locked in that cabin, I might get to find out her name anyway.

The missing persons report from the police will surely list it.

For such a thing to exist would mean I'd kept her locked up in that cabin for a long time because people aren't reported missing quickly. Time needs to pass, at least enough time to make it apparent that something is wrong. At least twenty-four hours, but depending on the case, it could be more before the police are interested enough to look into it. Less time for a vulnerable person like a child but more for a responsible adult.

I doubt we're anywhere near the point of somebody contacting the police yet, unless that woman has a partner waiting for her at home, some poor sod who was as naïve as me as to the person he chose to be in a relationship with. If she has, it will be him who reports her missing but not if she's single. If she is, it might be a friend or work colleague who goes to the police, but that could take days. How many commitments she has over the next seventy-two hours will determine how long it takes for somebody to realise she is not showing up where she should be.

But what if she has no plans for the next few days? What if she is a bit of a loner who has broken from her usual ways to be with my husband? What if she wouldn't be missed by anybody else out here?

That thought is a slightly delicious one because it would mean I could keep her locked away for a long time. How long? Long enough to make her think that she might never get out would be enough.

I guess this was inevitable. This decision to make this last longer than just one night. I tried to convince myself that I was just acting out of anger and that I'd let them out after a few hours, once I'd calmed down a little bit. But that's not really my way, and I know it.

That's because this isn't the first time I've locked two people away.

It's certainly not the first time I've locked two cheats away.

I've got history when it comes to this. That woman in my back garden doesn't know it, and Dominic certainly doesn't know it, but I do. I know all about what it's like to turn a key in a lock and take control of someone else's life. The feelings of power, control and satisfaction. And the feelings of guilt, fear and regret. But they only really come later, so I won't dwell on them for now.

My first instinct was to lock that door when I caught them tonight, just like it was my first instinct the last time I caught somebody else up to no good.

That was many years ago now, but it's something I think about every day.

How can I forget it?

It was the time I lost my innocence.

It was the time I became forever guilty.

12

GRACE

TEN YEARS OLD

Why do they have to pick on me? There are so many other girls at this school. Why am I the only one getting teased and pushed in the corridors?

It's not fair. It's been going on for too long. I've told my parents and my teachers, but nothing has changed. My teachers said they would stop the bullies, but it doesn't seem to have worked. Mum has told me to try and ignore them and stay strong until it's sorted out, but that hasn't worked either. And Dad has urged me to stand up for myself and fight back if they continue to be mean to me, but that isn't who I am.

I just want to be left alone.

But it feels like the only way I'll be able to be by myself is if I get out of here.

I've spent lots of time daydreaming about sneaking out of school and running away to somewhere where the mean girls in my class won't be able to call me names or try and trip me up. Most of my daydreams involve me running away to a park or playground where nobody knows me, and I can relax without worrying about somebody trying to upset me. But all of my daydreams end with me getting caught by somebody who drags me back to school, and then I get in trouble with my teachers and my parents, putting me in an even worse situation than I was in before.

I don't want to get in trouble, and that's why I haven't tried running away from school yet. But I don't want to get bullied anymore, and that's why I keep imagining what it would be like to escape my classroom. And that's why after another horrible meeting with my bullies in the corridor before the last lesson before lunchtime, I decide to just go for it.

I'm going to sneak out of school.

And I know just where to go so that I won't get caught.

I can't go home because it's too risky. I might get seen by a neighbour, or one of my parents might leave work early and catch me. I also don't have a key, so I can't get inside anyway. I'd just be stuck in the back garden, and that won't be great. I can't go into town either because I know some other kids in my school have been caught before when they have sneaked out because their uniforms have given them away. But there is somewhere I could go. It's somewhere very quiet, far away from other adults, and best of all, I know where the key is to get inside.

My dad has a small shed next to a lake where he likes to go fishing at the weekends. I think he calls it an allotment or something like that, but I don't use that word because I can't really say it properly. So I just call it a shed. It's like the one in our back garden but a little bigger. There's not much inside it. Just some fishing rods and some tubs of creepy crawlies that Dad says he needs because that's how he attracts the fish. I don't like fishing. I think it's really boring. But I do like that shed. I like how quiet it is there.

Nobody else is ever around.

I've been three times with Dad before, and we've never seen anybody else in all that time. I think that's why Dad likes it too. He says he goes there to get away from it all, whatever that means. I asked him if he wanted to get away from me once, but he just laughed and said no. Then I asked him if he wanted to get away from Mum, but he didn't say no to that as quickly.

Then he told me to promise not to tell Mum about the shed.

Dad says the shed is a secret from Mum because he doesn't want her to know how much money he paid for it. But he let me in on the secret because I think he wanted to cheer me up when he found me crying in my bedroom one night while I was upset about the bullies. He told me that I needed to stay strong and if I did, he would take me somewhere cool, somewhere nobody else knows about, and that sounded very exciting, so I stopped crying, and then he told me all about the secret place.

We went there the weekend after. Dad told Mum that he was taking me to the park, but he took me to the shed instead. I was a bit disappointed when I first saw it because there were no sweets there or swings to play on, but I was just happy to be with Dad, and he seemed to love the shed. He showed me around it, but it didn't take long. Then he put two little camping chairs outside the shed, beside the water, and told me to sit beside him before he showed me how he tried to catch fish.

I watched him put one of those creepy crawlies onto the hook at the end of his fishing rod before it disappeared into the water. Then we just sat and waited for ages and ages until something happened. Dad said that sometimes nothing ever happened, which sounded boring, but it did that day, and I was amazed when he lifted his fishing rod up, and there was a flapping fish on the other end of it.

I asked him what he was going to do with it, and he said he was going to put it back in the water because that's what he always did. I was glad about that because I didn't want the fish to die, and as it swam away, I wondered what it would tell all its friends when it got back to them. I remember wondering if the fish had more friends than me. But I didn't need friends because I had Dad, who seemed very pleased about that fish, and I was pleased for him.

That was a really nice day, and I have enjoyed the other two times I have been to that shed. It's nice just to sit with Dad and have a secret with him. I have secrets with Mum too, like when she gives me extra biscuits after dinner, so it's good that I have equal secrets with them both now.

I've decided that shed is where I am going to go today. Nobody will be there, and I can use the key under the plant pot behind the shed to open the door and go inside. I bet I could stay there all afternoon, and nobody would find me.

Dad says he likes the shed because it's an escape.

Now it's going to be my escape.

I sneak out of school at lunchtime. It's quite easy because all the other kids are busy playing games, and all the teachers are standing around talking, and nobody notices me walk around the side of the building until I'm out of sight. Then all I have to do is climb over the gate, and I am out. The gate is quite high, and it's scary when I'm on top of it, but I keep calm and make it over. I scratch my leg on one of the sharp edges of the gate as I go over, but I don't cry because I'm staying strong like Dad told me to be.

Now I'm out, and I feel so much better already just for being away from the school. I start running down the street, hoping that nobody out here will see me, before I leave the street and run through the park, sneaking through the trees and bushes until I get to the large field that used to have cows in but doesn't anymore. Mum and Dad said the farmer sold the cows, and that made me sad at the time, but I'm not sad now because it's easier to get through the field without looking out for all those animals.

I can see the roofs of all the houses on the estate in the distance. It's the estate where my house is, but I'm not going there now. I head in the opposite direction, cutting across the field until I reach the small stream that leads to the lake. I run across the bridge over the stream and hear my feet stamping loudly on the wooden floor before I see the lake up ahead.

It's a sunny day, and there are lots of flies buzzing about near the water. But there are no people here, and that's good. I pass two other sheds on the way to Dad's, but they have always been empty when I've been here before, and they are empty now. Dad's shed is on the other side of this lake, the farthest one away from the bridge and the only one that can't be seen from this side of the water because it is shielded by some bushes. That makes it a perfect hiding place, and as I get closer, I am excited about being one of the few people in town who knows about this place. I bet that's why Dad likes it too. Nobody comes here but us.

It's our secret. He told me about it to make me forget about the bullies. And now that I am here by myself, it has worked. I don't care about the bullies now because they can't get me here. Nobody can. I have this place all to myself.

And then I see that the door to the shed is open.

I stop running when I realise that somebody must already be inside it. Who is it? Dad? It must be because he's the only other person who would come here. But he shouldn't be here now. He should be at work. So what is he doing? Is he here to go fishing? Maybe. But if he is then I can't let him see me because he'll know I've snuck out of school then, and I'll get in trouble.

So what do I do?

I can't believe my bad luck. Now I have to make another plan. I'll have to go somewhere else. But where? I have no idea, so I hide behind one of the bushes next to the shed while I think about it. That's when I hear a voice inside the shed. But it's not Dad's. It's somebody else's. A woman's voice.

Is it Mum?

I don't think so. It doesn't sound like her.

So who is it?

I'm worried now that somebody has broken into Dad's shed and might be trying to steal all his things, so I decide to creep up to the door and try and peep inside to check.

I hear the woman's voice again as I get nearer to the door, and then she laughs. Is she laughing because she thinks she isn't going to get caught here? If so then she's wrong because I'm going to catch her right now, and then I'm going to tell Dad that somebody was in his shed who shouldn't have been. He won't be mad at me for leaving school then. He'll be glad I was here to catch the other person.

And then I hear Dad's voice too.

He is here.

What is he doing? And who is he with?

I reach the door and see the key is in the lock. It's the key I should have found under the plant pot, but it's already been used before I got here. And when I look inside, I see why.

Dad is inside the shed.

He's kissing a woman.

A woman who isn't Mum.

Neither of them have seen me by the door, and I keep watching them to see what happens, but they don't stop kissing, so eventually, I have to do something.

'Dad?'

They both stop and see me in the doorway, and when they do, they both look afraid, as if I've just caught them and not the other way around. I'm the one who has left school early. So why are the adults more nervous than me?

'Grace! What are you doing here?' Dad cries, and suddenly he looks angry, which makes me scared.

That's why I slam the door to the shed closed before he can get to me. I don't want to get in trouble for this.

To make sure, I turn the key in the lock.

Dad and that woman are stuck in the shed now.

I could open the door or leave it closed.

But whatever happens next, I think I'm going to be in trouble either way.

13

DOMINIC

I'm so cold. Kamilla is too. I can see her shaking slightly as she sits beside me, both our backs to the heater as we try to soak in the last bit of warmth that it might be radiating. But it's a futile task because the power in this cabin went off over an hour ago, and the heater is cold to the touch, meaning we're wasting our time sitting so close to it now. But we're still trying, just like I'm still trying the door handle on occasion, as well as calling outside to see if my wife is there and might be willing to let us out.

So far, no luck.

Grace must know how cold we are, yet she continues to torment us, and that's why I'm now starting to have a hard time telling Kamilla to be quiet when she calls my wife a crazy person. This is getting to the point where it is indefensible from Grace's perspective. Keeping us in here all night out in the cold is far beyond the realm of what could be considered an appropriate response to catching your partner cheating. Yet still this nightmare goes on, and as I see the first light of dawn beginning to crest on the horizon, I can scarcely believe we are entering a new day while we're still trapped in this cabin at the bottom of the garden.

Kamilla has stopped protesting for now, although that's only because she closed her eyes half an hour ago in an attempt to get some sleep. I'm not sure she has quite managed to drop off yet, but she has stubbornly refused to open her eyes either way, just like my wife has stubbornly refused to allow this stalemate of ours to end. But with more and more sunlight appearing, this has to end soon. For all the craziness of the last several hours in our private lives, mundane normality must resume. Kamilla, Grace and I all have jobs to go to. It's a Friday, and we'll be expected to be at our workstations by nine o'clock at the latest, sending emails, answering phone calls and doing whatever else we have to do today to continue to earn a living.

All that means Grace can't keep us here much longer. She will have to leave soon to go to her office, and she won't do that without first unlocking this cabin and letting us out. The hard part then will be convincing Kamilla to go to her office and not the police station, but hopefully, I can do that.

Hopefully, despite how it has started, this can end up being a fairly normal Friday after all.

I think about closing my eyes and trying to get some rest too, and my eyelids are certainly heavy enough for me to think that sleep might be a possibility, but I don't do it. With the glow from the window getting lighter by the minute, I decide to stand up and take another look outside now that I'll be able to see a lot more than I could a few hours ago. When I do look out, I see the burn pile in the middle of the garden.

But I also see my wife.

She is clearing it up.

I go to knock on the glass but pause because I will wake Kamilla if I do, and I don't need her to start shouting again. That hesitation allows me to take an extra moment to watch my wife at work, and as I do, I see how calmly and precisely she is moving as she shovels the pile of ashes into our garden waste bin. Surprisingly, her movements are not the hurried, frantic movements of a woman at war with herself, her husband and his mistress and the reality of what she has done. Rather, they are the movements of someone who is completely in control of this situation. If I didn't know any better, I'd say she is just ticking off another job on her To-Do list today.

Put a few dirty plates in the dishwasher.

Make a quick grocery list for the supermarket later.

Clear up the ashes from the burn pile I created in the middle of the night.

Get ready for another day of work.

Oh, and at some point today, I should probably let my prisoners out of that cabin.

It's haunting to see Grace behaving this way. She's so assured, acting like this isn't the wildest thing she has ever done in her life. But of course it is. I've been married to her for so many years now, I know everything there is to know about her. Sure, she can be a little impulsive and stubborn and get angry on occasion, but show me one woman who doesn't display those traits and emotions every now and again. And I know she had a slightly troubled upbringing and is still not on speaking terms with her mother, but not all families are perfect. Mine certainly isn't.

I want to speak to my wife now, make her see sense, try and find some of that woman I know and love that I'm sure is still inside of her somewhere. But I don't want there to be any distractions when I do. I need Kamilla to stay sleeping so that she doesn't get in the way of me trying to communicate directly with my wife. I won't be able to do that by banging on this window or shouting through the door. But what if there is another way of me communicating with Grace?

A more discreet way.

Like writing her a note.

I have paper and a pen on my desk, so I decide that I'm going to use those things to hopefully bring this nightmare to a swift end. I'll write Grace a note, one in which I get out all my apologies, regrets and future assurances of being a better husband and one that she can read quietly, calmly and without interference from Kamilla.

That will work, won't it?

Once written, I could just push it under this door, and Grace can pick it up and read it. I don't need to beg loudly or bang on anything now because that clearly doesn't get me anywhere. Subtleness is the way forward for me today, and with that plan of attack decided upon, I sit down in the chair and start writing.

Dear Grace,

I am so sorry for what I have put you through. You don't deserve any of this, and while it's already obvious, I will remind you again that none of this is your fault. I am the idiot here. I am the one who has

screwed things up. And I am the one who deserves to be punished.

I completely understand that you are angry and upset, and you have every right to not want to be near me at this time. So feel free to kick me out of the house, and I will give you all the time in the world that you need before you might entertain the idea of letting me try and explain myself to you in person. But please, try and see that keeping us locked away in here is not the answer. We deserve disgust and dismay but not imprisonment, starvation, dehydration and potential hypothermia. Please let us out. Neither of us in here want retribution. We just want to go to the bathroom, go to work, feel safe again. But that can't happen unless you unlock this door. So please do that, Grace. Please.

And once again, I am sorry for what I have done. If you will let me, I will spend the rest of my life trying to make it up to you. But if not, then I understand.

It won't change how I feel. I still love you.

Believe me when I say that.

Dominic xxx

I stare at the letter I have just composed and re-read it several times to make sure it has the right tone. I'm tempted to edit it and write more, or maybe I should write less, but after five minutes, I decide that it's the best I can do and put my pen down. Now all I need to do is deliver this letter to my wife, so I go over to the locked door and kneel beside it.

Carefully folding the letter in half, I slide it underneath the door until it disappears from my view, before I go over to the window to see if Grace has noticed what I have just done. It looks like she has because she has stopped shovelling the ashes and is now making her way down towards the cabin.

My heart beats a little faster at the thought that I might finally be about to make my exit from this cabin, and while Grace leaves my line of vision, I know it's only because she has bent down to pick up the letter on the floor. She soon reappears as she unfolds the letter and begins to read it, and I wait patiently as she devours every word.

It takes a little while, and I guess it's because she is re-reading it almost as much as I did, but she is eventually finished with it because she lowers the letter before looking at me through the window.

I do my best impression of a wounded animal, hoping my puppy-dog eyes and sorrowful expression will add greater depth to the letter and seal the deal on getting that key out of Grace's pocket and into the lock it belongs in. But it doesn't quite work out that way because Grace just turns and walks back to the house, and I feel nauseous as I watch her go because it looks like even this hasn't worked, and there is still no end in sight.

I want to bang on the glass and shout again as I watch my wife go back into the house, but I don't because the kitchen door doesn't close behind her, giving me some hope that she might be making an appearance in the garden again any moment now.

Maybe she left the key inside and has gone in to get it. That could be it. The letter might still have worked. This might all be over soon.

And then Grace reappears, striding out of the house and back down towards the cabin, and she is walking with a definiteness of purpose that makes me feel ever more confident that she is about to do what she should have done several hours ago.

She is going to do the right thing.

She reaches the cabin, still with my letter in her hand, and I nod my head at her as if to give her the final push to let me out. But she doesn't do that. Instead, she just folds my letter in half again before sliding it under the door, back the way it came.

I stare at the piece of paper on the cabin floor and don't really understand why it has been returned to me, but when I look outside, I see Grace, and this time, she is the one nodding.

Taking that as a hint that she has sent me a note of her own, I pick up the paper and unfold it, noticing immediately that she has written something of her own in red ink just below the words I wrote so carefully in black ink a few minutes ago.

It's a short, simple statement and not at all the one I was hoping to receive. It doesn't display the type of thought and desperation that I conveyed in my own writing, nor does it offer a way forward like my message did. Instead, it reads very bluntly, leaving little room for misinterpretation or hope.

You men are all the same.

14

GRACE

Dawn heralds a new day and with it, the chance to start afresh. Everybody witnessing this latest sunrise has the same chance as each other and that is to forget about yesterday and focus on the new opportunities that lie ahead. Everybody except me, of course, because I can't forget about what happened.

That's why Dominic and that woman are still in the cabin.

My husband, bless him, wrote me a note a little while ago telling me how sorry he was in a desperate attempt to get me to let him out so he could start his own day anew. But I am pretty certain that I have let him know where he stands in no uncertain terms by responding to that note with a message of my own.

I told him that all men were the same, and unfortunately, my grim experiences with the opposite sex prove that to be true.

My husband is a cheat.

Just like my father was.

Why can't I have had one good man in my life? Is that too much to ask? At least I've been able to do something about it. Some men might see women as weak, but there's nothing weak about me, and Dominic is going to find out just how strong I am today because while he remains in that cabin, I am going to go to work and get on with my life in a display of strength and resolve that will surely leave him scratching his head as to how he could ever have decided to test me in the first place.

After pushing the note back under the cabin door, I went back into the house and got dressed. The weather forecast says it will be quite warm today, so I've opted for a blouse and skirt, nothing too revealing but something that will help me keep comfortable in the mild weather. Dominic and that woman are lucky that it's only cold at night. But that's as much luck as they're going to get today.

I make myself a coffee and pour it into my flask, so I can enjoy it on the drive into the office. I'm due at my desk in forty minutes, and it's a thirty-minute drive, so I have a little time to play with before I have to leave the house. Taking advantage of that, I put on a little music to give me a mental boost. Nothing too heavy for this time of the day, just a little country song I like that always makes me feel good. There might not be many people in this part of the UK who listen to music made in Tennessee, USA, but I am one of them, and as it always does, the song improves my mood and has me ready to tackle the day ahead.

By the time it's finished playing, I have car keys in my hand and my hot flask in the other, and as I reach the front door, I only pause to smile to myself. It's Friday, a day when most people are happy because the weekend is almost here, and they can have a break.

But the weekend will hold no respite for the couple out in the garden.

I'm going to have to take Dominic's car to get to work today on account of my vehicle still being parked at my office where I left it yesterday before attending the networking event. But it's no problem because Dominic sure as hell won't be using his car today.

The air is pleasant and warm as I step outside, and I'm just thinking about how I might get a rare opportunity to drive with the windows down in the car when I hear a noise to my left.

Glancing towards the house next to mine, I see my neighbour, Frank, coming towards me. He's cutting across the trimmed patch of grass that separates our properties, even though Dominic has politely asked him in the past not to walk over it because a worn-out trail was starting to reveal itself, and that hardly looks good. But Frank has either forgotten about that friendly request or he is choosing to completely ignore it because he trots across the grass as if it's a concrete path before giving me a smile and a wave.

'Morning, neighbour! How's it going?'

I force a smile onto my face because I'm not particularly happy to see him and not just because I currently have two people locked up at the back of my house. It's also because I need to get going if I'm to make it to work on time, but Frank has always been a chatterer, and I'm wondering how long he is going to hold me up today.

'Good morning, Frank. I'm good, thank you. How are you?'

'Great! It's supposed to be nice today. A mild autumn day, what a treat. It's quite warm already, isn't it? Much warmer than it was in the night. I was chilly, weren't you?'

I nod my head before closing and locking my front door, working quickly to hopefully show Frank that I don't really have the time for chit-chat this morning. But he doesn't get the hint because he keeps on talking to me anyway.

'Are you ready for the weekend?'

'Yeah, of course. You?'

'I've been ready since Monday afternoon, I think!'

He laughs loudly at his own joke before asking me what I have planned for this Saturday and Sunday.

'Not much. Just a quiet one for me.'

'Fair enough. It's good to just unwind at the end of the week, isn't it? I'm always saying to Maggie that we should take it a little easier on weekends. But she's always booking us in for so many things. Dinners and drinks with friends and all that kind of stuff. It's all good fun, but I'd just like to put my feet up every now and again, you know what I mean? Sometimes I end the weekend more exhausted than when I started it!'

Brilliant, do I really need to know this?

I smile again politely before heading for my car. But Frank doesn't leave it there.

'How's Dominic doing? Has he got any plans this weekend?'

I freeze at the mention of my husband's name, still a couple of feet away from my vehicle. Why did he have to bring him up? Why couldn't he just have wished me a good day and left it at that? Now I'm going to have to make up an excuse about what my husband is doing this weekend.

But what can I say?

'Erm…he's fine, thanks for asking.'

'Good. So what's he doing? Any plans? If not, I was wondering if he fancied a beer tomorrow afternoon. Nothing too wild, just a quick catch-up. I feel like we haven't had a drink in a while.'

I don't say that the reason Dominic hasn't had a drink with Frank for a while is due to the fact that he finds him an insufferable bore because that would be extremely rude, so I just smile again and say that he's been very busy.

'Ahh, he's been in that cabin of his, I suspect,' Frank chuckles. 'He spends a lot of time in there, doesn't he?'

More than I'd like you to know.

'Yeah.'

'Is he in there right now?'

Frank knows all about my husband's workspace at the bottom of the garden. What he doesn't know is that it has a new purpose now, and he can never know that.

'He's not, actually,' I say as my mind races for something to tell Frank that will ensure my annoying neighbour doesn't decide to try and knock on the cabin door while I'm out at work all day. One might think that a person wouldn't just enter the back garden of their neighbour while they were out, but Frank has occasionally taken it upon himself to waltz straight in through the side gate and try and say hello to Dominic that way, rather than just popping his head over the garden fence like a normal person would. The thought of him doing such a thing today worries me greatly, so I need to make sure it doesn't even cross Frank's mind.

'What's he up to?' Frank asks.

'He's working away,' I lie, but I'm satisfied that it should be enough to stop Frank thinking about my husband and the possibility of a beer this weekend.

'Is he? Where's he gone?'

'Up north. Some conference thing.'

'On a weekend? That's no fun.'

'Yeah, he wasn't happy about it. But he didn't have much choice.'

'But his car is here.'

Yes, it is. Nice of you to notice, Frank.

'A colleague picked him up.'

'Oh, I see. What about your car?'

'It's at my office. A friend brought me home last night.'

'Wow, you and Dominic sure do lead busy lives.'

So says the street's number one busybody.

'Oh well, I guess I'll see him when he's back,' Frank says with a shrug. 'When is that, exactly?'

'Erm, a couple of days.'

It's a fairly vague reply, but I again try to wrap this conversation up by making another move towards the car. But as I get there and unlock it, Frank has one more thing to say, and it's clear he isn't finished being nosey yet.

'Forgive me if I'm mistaken but were you burning something last night?'

I take a sharp intake of breath as my mind races over the possibility that I might have been seen burning all those things in the back garden. But it would be impossible. Frank and Maggie's house doesn't overlook our garden, so they can't have seen me out there in the dead of night.

'It's just we were sleeping with the window open, and I smelt smoke. I was worried something was on fire, so I came out to the front of the house, but everything seemed okay. Then I wondered if it might have been in the back garden. But it seemed to stop quite quickly, so I wasn't sure.'

'Errr, yeah, it was me.'

'Oh, right. What was it?'

'It was a fire pit. We bought it last week. I was just trying it out to make sure that it worked.'

'So late at night?'

'I couldn't sleep.'

'I see. Well I guess it did work, if the smell of burning was anything to go by.'

'Yeah, it did.'

I really want to go. Please, just let me go.

'So how are those fire pits?' Frank asks, not letting this conversation end. 'Maggie and I have been toying with the idea of getting one. Are they worth it?'

'Yeah, I'd say so. I mean, we haven't used it properly yet, but I think it will be good.'

'Great. Maybe you can give us some tips when you've had a little more use out of it.'

‘Will do. I really have to get going now.’

‘Of course. Sorry for keeping you. Have a good day at the office. It’ll be five o’clock before you know it.’

I smile and wave Frank off as I get in the car and start the engine, but I don’t make any attempt to reverse until I have seen him walk back across the grass to his property. I want to make sure he is going back to his business in his house and not still interfering with the business in mine. But he is, and as he opens his front door and goes back inside, I give him another wave before finally exiting my driveway and getting on the road.

That was a risky moment, but I think I came through it okay. It wasn’t all a waste of time either because now my neighbours think Dominic is away for the weekend, it means they won’t be wondering why they haven’t seen him over the next few days. That has bought me some time, I guess, at least around here. But other people will be wondering where Dominic is, mainly his colleagues when he fails to log on to his employer’s server soon. That’s why the next lie I tell involves me making a phone call to his office to speak to the receptionist there and let her know that Dominic is feeling under the weather today after eating something that hasn’t agreed with him.

It’s easy to find the phone number for his office online because it’s just a quick Google search after I pull over by the side of the road, and the woman at the other end of the line thanks me for my call and sends her best wishes to my husband, before I hang up quickly. As I put my phone down and carry on driving, I try not to wonder if that receptionist is another female that my husband might have been tempted by in the past. But I can't think like that. I can't let his philandering ways keep bringing me down.

The closer I get to my own office, the better I am feeling about things. I can do this. I can get through the day without anybody realising that something is wrong in my life. Of course, my confidence, like most people's, comes from experience. This won't be the first time I have to act normal while knowing somebody is locked away and only I have the key. I can draw on what happened in the past to help me now.

I can just remind myself what I did when I was a child.

If I could manage this when I was ten, I can surely manage it now.

15

GRACE

TEN YEARS OLD

The first thing I did after locking my dad and that woman in the shed was go back to school. I didn't know what else to do. All I knew was that I wanted to get away from that place. The place where I had done something that might get me in trouble now.

Nobody at school noticed I was gone. I wasn't gone for long, but still, not a single person noticed. Not any of the teachers and certainly not any of the other kids in my class. They never notice me. But today, that is okay. I was back for the end of lunchtime, having ran all the way to school from that shed. The faster I ran, the more I got scared about how much trouble I was in, and that made me try to run even faster. I was out of breath by the time I sneaked back into school, and I'm still sweating a bit now as I sit here in the classroom and try to concentrate on what Mrs Smith is saying.

But I can't.

All I can think about is Dad and what will happen when I let him out.

I hate being in trouble, so that's why I try to stay out of it. But I'm in it now. Lots of trouble. But I couldn't help it. I got so scared and angry and confused seeing Dad with that woman. I just locked them in. I didn't think. I just did it.

The afternoon goes slowly, even more slowly than usual. Mrs Smith notices I'm daydreaming because she says my name two times, once to test me on a Maths question and another time to ask me what she just said. I just sat and stared at her hopelessly both times until she shook her head at me and moved on. A few of the girls in my class laughed at me then, but I didn't care. I just wanted class to end.

By the time I'm finished with school, Dad has been locked in that shed for three hours.

I wait for Mum as I always do by the school gates. I watch a lot of the other kids get collected by their parents before me, and none of them say goodbye to me as they go. Finally, Mum appears, rushing as always, saying sorry for being late but work was busy. Now we're in the car, and she's driving me home while asking me about my day. But I'm making sure not to say anything.

'What did you learn today?'

Nothing.

'Have you got any homework?'

Nothing.

'Is everything okay? Has something happened?'

Nothing.

Mum gets annoyed at me and asks why I'm not talking to her, but I just tell her that I'm tired and yawn to try and prove it.

'Okay, well, if that's the case, it's early to bed for you tonight. No TV after your dinner. Just a shower and then straight to sleep.'

Such a suggestion would usually be awful, but I don't even argue with it. I just stare out of the window and think about Dad.

As we get closer to home, I think about how I might try and tell Mum what I've done when we get to our house. But I just don't know how to say any of it without getting myself in trouble. Leaving school. Finding Dad with someone else. Locking them in. That's all bad news. Mum will be upset about the other woman, and I don't want to make her cry. She'll also be angry at me, and then she will go to let Dad out, and he'll be even angrier.

I can't do it.

Not yet, anyway.

We get home, and Mum tells me to make sure I have everything that I need in my schoolbag for tomorrow because she doesn't want a repeat of this morning when I couldn't find anything I needed and almost made us late. I do as I'm told, staying quiet as Mum goes into the kitchen and turns on the radio. Then I hear her singing, and it makes me feel like I still can't say anything about Dad yet because she is happy, and telling her will only make her sad.

Mum always sings when she's in a good mood. Dad says it sounds like somebody strangling a cat, but when I asked what that meant, Mum just told me to ignore him and that if I wanted to sing then nobody should ever stop me. But I never really sing.

I guess that's because I'm never really happy.

I try and eat the spaghetti and sauce that Mum has made me for my dinner, but I'm not hungry. I just feel sick, and the later it gets, the worse I feel. It's been five hours now since I locked Dad in that shed. And worst of all, Mum still thinks he will be home from work soon.

Dad always comes in the house at six o'clock, and the time on the microwave says that it's 5:47. Mum doesn't know what I know. She doesn't know that Dad won't be here when he should be.

'What's wrong? Why aren't you eating your dinner?' Mum asks me, and I stop staring at the digital clock that now says 5:51 and look down at the food in my bowl.

'I'm not hungry.'

'Why not?'

I shrug.

'Did you eat your lunch?'

I nod.

'Have you eaten anything since then?'

'No.'

'Then why aren't you hungry? Are you ill?'

Mum touches my forehead and frowns.

'I'm okay. I'm just not hungry.'

'Hmmm. You don't have a temperature. What about your stomach? Have you been to the toilet more than usual today?'

'No.'

'Then I don't understand why you aren't eating. You like spaghetti, don't you?'

'Yeah.'

'So what's wrong?'

I feel tears starting to well up in my eyes, and I almost start crying right in front of Mum. But I don't want to cry here. I want to do it when I'm alone in my bedroom where nobody can see me.

'Nothing.'

Mum hasn't noticed the tears yet, and I quickly wipe my eyes when she turns away.

'Well unless you can give me a good reason why you're not eating then I'm afraid you're going to have to sit there all night until your plate is empty.'

'But Mum!'

'Your Dad will be home soon. He'll want to know why you haven't eaten anything either.'

I almost tell her that he won't be home, but I don't. I just pick up my fork again and try to finish my spaghetti.

Mum watches me closely before asking if any of the girls have been picking on me again at school. They have, but I shake my head because I'm not even thinking about them anymore. Mum seems pleased about that, though she isn't singing along to the radio now. And then the clock on the microwave says 5:59, and I feel like I'm going to be sick again.

I watch it and keep watching it, waiting for it to show 6:00. It takes ages, and I start to think the clock might be broken, but it eventually changes.

Now it's the time Dad usually gets home.

And soon, Mum will be wondering where he is.

I manage to eat just over half of my food before I persuade Mum that I'm really full, and after she checks my bowl, she shrugs and takes it away from the table.

‘Time for your shower,’ she says after that, and I follow her upstairs, trying not to look at the front door as I go because it will only remind me of how Dad isn’t going to be coming through it tonight.

I think about how I’ll tell Mum what happened with Dad after my shower, but I don’t, and as I wrap the towel around myself and stand shivering in the bathroom, I see Mum check her watch.

‘Your Dad’s late,’ she says, before telling me to go to my room while she gets the hairdryer.

I stand by my bed, cold and still a little wet, as I wait for her to get back, and when she does, she asks me why I’m not putting my pyjamas on.

‘Honestly, I don’t know what has gotten into you tonight, but I wish you’d tell me,’ Mum says before she turns the hairdryer on.

I usually like it when Mum dries my hair because it makes me feel girly as she runs her hands through my long locks and tells me that I am going to be very pretty when I grow up. But I don’t like it tonight. I don’t look at my reflection in the mirror as she works on my hair. I just stare at the carpet and think about Dad.

‘Okay, are you sure you don’t want to tell me what’s wrong?’ Mum asks me one more time, but I shake my head again, so she says I should just get into bed and sleep if I’m still tired.

I’m relieved to finally get under my duvet, and I clutch onto it tightly as I lie underneath it, comforted by it. Things always feel a bit better when I’m in bed. This is my safe place. Nothing can hurt me here. No monsters. No bullies. No trouble from what I did to Dad.

'Goodnight, darling,' Mum says to me after she gives me a kiss and strokes my hair. 'I hope you're feeling better tomorrow.'

She goes to leave, but just before she does, I try and tell her what I've been wanting to say all night. But all that comes out is a soft squeak, and Mum doesn't even hear it, before she turns off my light and closes my bedroom door.

I can't stop crying once I'm alone in the dark. I bury my face in my pillow and feel it getting wet, and I don't stop until I have no more tears left to cry. When I do lift my head up, I can hear my Mum. She's talking to somebody downstairs.

Who is it? Is it Dad? *Has he got out of the shed and made it home?*

I sneak out of bed and open my door, before creeping towards the top of the stairs and hearing Mum's voice again.

'Where are you? If you're working late then that's fine, but just let me know. Call me when you get this. I love you.'

I see Mum walk through the hallway below me then with her mobile phone. I guess she just phoned Dad to see where he was and left him a message. He mustn't have answered his phone but then I remember Dad told me that there is no signal at the shed, which is another reason he likes it there. But because he hasn't answered, Mum knows something is definitely wrong now. But she still doesn't know what.

I should go down and tell her. This is the time to do it. I should stop her worrying. I also should help Dad get out of that shed because it's dark outside now, and he might be getting scared. But I'm scared too, and I also know that if Dad hadn't been in there with that woman then none of this would have happened.

This is his fault. He made me do this. I'm sure everything will be okay. He's a grown up. He'll get out, and he might not say anything when he gets home. He might just pretend like it didn't happen. I could pretend too. I'd like that.

I wish it was yesterday and none of this had happened. Not today. *Today has been a bad day.*

I stand at the top of the stairs for a long time, still thinking about going down to talk to Mum. But then I turn back to my bedroom, and without trying to think about it anymore, I decide that I'll do something tomorrow if Dad isn't home by then. But I'm sure he will be. He'll get out. If he doesn't then I'll tell Mum everything. But right now, I am tired, so I'm going to try and go to sleep.

I hope everything will be better in the morning.

It has to be, right?

16

DOMINIC

I decided not to show Kamilla the note that Grace and I had written to each other when she woke up. I didn't need her to see how pathetic I had sounded when I'd begged Grace to let us out, nor did I want her to see the blunt response that my wife had delivered in return. That's why I screwed the note up and tossed it into the wastepaper bin under my desk before slumping into my office chair and trying to figure out a new way out of this. But by the time Kamilla had stirred, I still had nothing.

'What time is it?' Kamilla asks me as she rubs her eyes and looks towards the window.

'I don't know. The sun came up a while ago. Could be seven. Eight. Nine.'

'Nine? I need to be at work!'

'You and me both. But I don't think that's going to happen today.'

'Where the hell is she?'

Kamilla is at the window now, looking out at the garden and the closed back door to the house. I don't bother mentioning to her why that door is probably closed. It's because Grace will have locked it just before she went to work.

One of us will be fulfilling our professional duties today. But how my wife can possibly concentrate during a day in the office after what she has done is beyond me.

At least I presume she is at work. She could still be in the house, I suppose, but I believe I heard the sound of a car engine earlier, so that could have been her leaving. Guessing it was, I put the time at around half-past eight because that's usually when Grace leaves for the office. From there, I did my best to try and count in multiples of sixty as a way of keeping track of the minutes. But I lost count somewhere along the way, no doubt a combination of my extreme fatigue, gnawing hunger and general anxiety about what my wife is doing to us. I also realised that my wife could purposely have left at a different time than usual to throw me off. After all this, that definitely seems like something she might do.

'I don't know,' I say in reply to Kamilla's question about my wife's whereabouts, opting to keep the sound of the car engine to myself too because it won't make her feel any better to know that Grace isn't even around anymore.

'I need to get to the office. She's going to get me fired!'

'Calm down. You're not going to get fired for missing one day.'

'I might do. I'm only a temp!'

'It'll be okay.'

'That's easy for you to say. You're a full employee. You have all the rights. They can't just replace you. But I'm dispensable.'

'You're right, I am a full employee, which is why it will be far worse for me to not report for my duties, unlike you, who I doubt anyone will notice is missing at all.'

I didn't mean for that to come out as mean as it sounded, and I try to take it back instantly, but Kamilla is hurt, and worse, she's angry at me now.

'How dare you! Do you know how hard I work at that place to try and prove myself so they might consider making me permanent? I bet I work harder than you!'

'I'm sorry.'

'Are you? Why would you say that?'

'I didn't mean it.'

I really don't have time to indulge in a childish argument now, although I'm aware the fact I snapped at Kamilla and chose to attack her position in the company is a sign that deep down, I perhaps don't respect her, at least professionally, as much as I should do. I'm not so shallow as to have seen her merely as an attractive woman who can satisfy my desires; I know there is far more to her than good looks. She's clever and funny and has a good work ethic. I just said the wrong thing through lack of sleep; she snapped back thanks to her own fatigue, and now we're wasting time on this nonsense instead of figuring out a way to get out of here.

'It should go without saying,' Kamilla hisses at me, 'but when this is over, we're done. You hear me?'

I should apologise again, maybe say we'll talk it all through later when we're in a different situation. But I don't. I just pick the easy thing to say.

'Fine,' I reply, and I throw in a casual shrug to add more weight to my response.

Kamilla looks like she expected me to object to her idea a little more, probably wondering how a guy like me could just let a younger woman go without a fight, but I'm not in the mood for being possessive. What I am in the mood for is some fresh air.

'Stand back,' I say as I get off my chair and pick it up by the armrests.

'What are you doing?'

'Getting desperate.'

I urge Kamilla to move away from the window again, and this time she does as I advise, giving me a clear shot at that extra-strong pane of glass that is our best way out of here.

'Do you think it'll work?' Kamilla asks, but I ignore her, choosing instead to put all my energy into holding the chair in the position that will give me the best chance of throwing it hard. I've never thrown a chair before, nor have I ever seen anyone else throw one, and there's probably a good reason for that.

They're not the easiest things to throw.

'One, two, three!'

Giving it everything I've got, I hurl the chair at the window, but it's a poor attempt at a throw because I'm not strong, nor am I particularly coordinated, and only a fraction of the chair hits the glass. Most of it just hits the side of the cabin beneath the windowpane before loudly impacting the floor, and all I seem to have got for my troubles there is breaking one of the armrests on the chair.

‘Well, that was rubbish,’ Kamilla tells me, not that I needed any feedback on my performance. I could have given it a poor grade myself.

‘I’ll try again,’ I say, picking the chair up, but it’s even harder now because the broken armrest just swings limply as I hold it, giving me even less purchase on the awkwardly shaped object.

‘No, we need something else. Something easier to throw. Like this!’

Kamilla picks up the wine bottle from the desk and launches it at the window, barely giving me a chance to get out of the way as it whizzes past my head, but despite putting all her effort into it, the bottle doesn’t even come close to breaking through the window. It could have done some serious damage to my skull, though and of course, it shatters on impact, sending shards of glass to the floor while half the bottle rolls across the wood, its jagged edges meaning it’s best to be avoided unless one wants to risk cutting themselves on it.

‘What the hell did you do that for?’ I cry, but she doesn’t seem bothered about almost knocking me unconscious, nor coating the floor with glass while we stand here in bare feet.

‘Why did you have to get such strong glass?’ she moans, but I ignore that question because I’ve already answered before, instead focusing on trying to pick up as many of the pieces of glass as I can. But I know it’ll be impossible to get them all and before I know it, I’ve already stood on one piece and cut myself, small droplets of blood dripping from my injured foot onto the stained wood and causing it to turn a deep red.

I glare at Kamilla as I check my injury before telling her we'll have to be very careful about where we tread now. But she's already moved on to finding something else to throw against the window and I guess I might as well help her as that's our best way out of here.

Between us, we spend the next five minutes throwing anything we can get our hands on at the window, including heavy box files full of piles of paperwork, which only serves to litter the floor with said paperwork and very quickly, this once tidy cabin is starting to look like a mess. I throw a very cheap and unglamorous award I won over a decade ago for contributing to a successful project, and even a chunky paperweight, which I was slightly confident might do the trick. But none of them work. The guys who fitted the window really did deserve a bigger tip than the one I gave them.

I give up at that point, but Kamilla has one more thing to try.

The wastepaper bin.

I see the screwed-up note that I wrote to Kamilla fall out of it as she turns it upside down before she throws it against the glass. Surprise, surprise, that doesn't work either. All it has done is put the note out in the open, and I do my best to try and kick the paper away into a corner of the cabin before Kamilla can unravel and read it, most likely out of nothing but sheer boredom. But she picks it up before I can get to it.

'What are the chances of this being the thing that breaks the glass?' she asks me jokingly, and I laugh nervously. But I'd be quite happy for her to throw it. Rather that than open it and read it.

The ball of paper remains in her hand as she looks around for something better to throw, but when she doesn't find it, she slumps down to the floor, her back against the cabin and her head shaking at all the wasted energy we have just produced.

Then she starts laughing.

'What's funny?' I ask, not seeing a joke anywhere in here.

'I'm just thinking about how my friends will react when I tell them this story the next time I see them. I mean, don't get me wrong, they've told me some crazy tales in their time from all the guys they have been involved with. But this will top them all. There's no way they will be able to beat this.'

Kamilla tosses the paper between her hands, still sniggering, and I watch the paper moving around while also wondering if it might be wishful thinking on her part to assume that she will eventually get out of here to tell her friends all about this. But I don't say anything. I just slump down against the wall opposite her and hold out my hand to receive a catch.

'Over here,' I say, hinting that I want her to throw me the ball of paper.

Kamilla stops tossing it between her hands and thinks about playing the game I have just suggested. Sure, it might seem childish to her, but what else is there to do here, right? I guess she realises that because she eventually throws it over to me, and once I catch it, I plan on keeping hold of it.

‘Throw it back,’ she says, but I shake my head.

‘Nah, I’ve think I’ve proved how bad I am at throwing things enough for one day.’

Kamilla rolls her eyes at that but doesn’t disagree, and we sit in silence for a few moments before she has another question for me.

‘Has your wife ever done anything like this before?’

‘Lock me and another woman in a cabin? No, this is the first time.’

‘Don’t get sarcastic with me. I’m being serious. Has she ever shown any tendencies for wanting to have control over you? Keep you restrained in any way?’

I go to shake my head and dismiss that notion, but then I remember something. I remember a time four years ago. Grace and I were away for the weekend together. I did something to annoy her.

And she responded in a slightly unusual way.

I’d almost forgotten all about it. It was weird at the time, but so much has happened since then. We never talked about it again, and I put it down to just one weird event in a relationship that was otherwise boringly normal. But now I think about it, it could have been a precursor to what has happened here.

‘What is it? What has she done before?’ Kamilla asks me, clearly noticing a change in my expression and figuring out that I have something to share with her.

So I do share it.

I tell her all about what happened the last time my wife got angry with me.

17

DOMINIC

FOUR YEARS AGO

Bath is a beautiful city. I've been here a couple of times before, once with my parents when I was a child to see the sights and once for a weekend with friends to explore the local pubs, but my third time in this popular part of Somerset is for purely romantic reasons.

I've swept my wife away for a two-day break, one that she had no idea about until she woke up on Saturday morning and saw two small bags of luggage already packed and waiting by the door. Grace was thrilled when I told her my plan, the one that included the hotel I had booked for us in Bath, as well as the fancy French restaurant I had made a reservation for on Saturday night. All she needed to do was agree to go with me, and we would be set.

Well, that wasn't strictly true. She also had to tell our next-door neighbour, Maggie, that she wouldn't be able to make the wine and cheese 'get-together' that evening that she was originally supposed to go to, but I didn't expect that to be too much of a problem. And so it proved as Grace went next door and told Maggie about her new plans for the weekend while I put the bags in the back of the car and made the final preparations for us to hit the road.

The journey along the motorway was problem-free, and our arrival in Bath went as I hoped it would. My wife gawked out of the passenger seat window at all the pretty, golden-coloured buildings that populate the city and contribute to it being a World Heritage Site, while I sat behind the wheel with a big smile on my face. It was her first time in the city, but Grace fell in love with Bath immediately, as most people who visit it do, and after we had checked in to the hotel and left our belongings in the spacious and expensive room, we had hit the streets to do some exploring.

But that was where things had started to go wrong.

Despite telling my boss that I would be busy all weekend and that he would have to find somebody else to help assist with the urgent project that needed to be delivered ahead of schedule this upcoming Monday, my phone started to ring.

And it wouldn't stop.

'I can't do it,' I stressed after I eventually answered a call. 'I'm sorry, but I'm away for the weekend with my wife. Give it to Gregg. He can help,' I urged my employer while talking quietly into my phone as Grace was window-shopping a little further down the street from me. I really didn't want her to hear that I was taking a work call because that would hardly be keeping in the spirit of a romantic getaway, would it? But despite my pleas, my boss wasn't hearing any of them.

'I've tried Gregg. And I've tried everybody else too. You're my last hope. Please, Dom, I need you to do this. I need you to look at the emails I've just sent you.

There are a couple of attachments. Go through them and let me know what you think while I work on putting out some other fire back here.'

'I can't.'

'Sorry, but I'm not asking you, Dom.'

'I don't believe this.'

'Neither do I. I'm in the office on a Saturday morning. Don't you think I'd rather be spending time with my own wife?'

'Damn it.'

'Look, I appreciate I'm asking a big favour of you, so I promise I'll make it up to you. This won't be forgotten about at bonus time, I'll see to that, and then you can spoil Grace all you want to, okay?'

I still felt like arguing and defending the value of my free time, as well as the importance of spending quality time with my wife, but like my boss had said, he wasn't asking me, and that meant he was telling me.

'Fine, I'll look at the emails, and I'll get back to you with my thoughts,' I growled down the phone before hanging up and shaking my head. Then I looked at Grace and tried to think of a way of telling her that instead of pleasantly wandering around Bath shopping, drinking and chatting away to each other, I was now going to have to go back to the hotel room and read some damn work emails.

As I feared, Grace didn't take it well.

'It was your idea to go away this weekend! I was quite happy to stay at home. I cancelled my wine and cheese night with Maggie for this. And now you're abandoning me?'

'I'm not abandoning you. It's just for a couple of hours. Three, tops. I'll go back, do this work and then come out and meet you. You can do some shopping or find a nice café for a slice of cake and a cup of tea.'

'I'm not sitting in a café on my own. And I'm not walking around Bath on my own either. I came here with you!'

'I know that, and I said I'm sorry, but this is urgent. It has to be done today. But I've been told I'll get rewarded at bonus time, so it's not all bad, right?'

The carrot of a financial reward is not met as well as I had hoped, and Grace just scoffs before telling me to do whatever I want and storming away from me, turning a corner and disappearing into the Saturday shopping crowd before I have another chance to try and smooth things over with her.

I rushed back to the hotel room to get started on my work straight away, but once there, I realised I had made a mistake in estimating how long it would take me to complete my task. The emails and their corresponding attachments were full of all sorts of issues, ones that meant I wouldn't be doing my job properly if I didn't raise them with my employer. So that's what I had to do. I had to make a list of each and every problem I saw in what was being proposed, something that was extremely time-consuming because it involved a lot of reading and re-reading tedious contracts and all of it on the small screen of my mobile phone.

With a banging headache, not to mention a stiff neck and tired eyes, I eventually compiled an appropriate email to send back to my boss, and when that was done,

I leapt out of my chair and rushed towards the hotel room door. My plan was to get out and find Grace as quickly as I could, but unfortunately for me, my wife found me first.

The door opened before I could get to it, and Grace walked in, still looking angry, although the two shopping bags she had with her gave me hope that her mood might have been lightened somewhat by a little retail therapy.

'Oh, you're back! I was just on my way out to meet you. What have you got there? Anything nice?'

I gestured towards the bags before trying to get a peek inside them, but Grace just swiped them away from me before tossing them down by her side of the bed and fixing me with a steely glare.

'Have you finished your work?'

'Yes, all done!'

'That's it? You're not going to get another phone call and suddenly have some more to do?'

'No, definitely not! That's it, I promise!'

My convincing tone and wide smile seemed to do the trick because Grace's stance softened then, and when she spoke next, she really surprised me.

'Okay, I think it's time for you to make it up to me. Get on the bed.'

'What?'

'You heard me.'

It took me a moment to get on the same wavelength as my wife, but once I had, I didn't waste any time in following her orders.

I lay down on the bed and patted the patch of duvet beside me for Grace to come and join me but before she did, she told me to start taking my clothes off. Again, I did as I was told, and by the time I was naked, I was wondering how I had somehow managed to turn what could have been a ruined weekend away into one that suddenly seemed to ooze passion and adventure.

Grace went into one of the shopping bags then, and when I asked her what she was doing, she responded by telling me that she was punishing me. I had no idea what she meant by that until I saw the handcuffs come out of the bag, and as she dangled them in front of me, my eyes must have gone as wide as a child's on Christmas morning.

'Are you serious?' I'd asked while fully hoping that she was, and when Grace nodded and told me to put my hands back against the bars of the bedframe, I was completely ready to receive my 'punishment'.

'We've never done anything like this before,' I noted, slightly worried that I was sounding a little giddy as I spoke but struggling to contain my excitement. But I wasn't wrong. While I had long been campaigning for a little more spontaneity between us in the bedroom, my wife had never demonstrated that she was interested in making our sex life any more adventurous than it already was, and it was far from adventurous. But as the handcuffs went around my wrists and the bars before tightening and locking, I was thinking about how Grace had finally realised that I had been right.

We needed more passion in our relationship.

And now it looked like we were going to have it.

'How do they feel? Nice and tight?' Grace asked me as she wiggled the handcuffs against my skin to test if they would hold me. But they definitely would, and I knew that because they were hurting my wrists slightly, not that I was going to say anything because the last thing I wanted to do was ruin the moment and mess up my one chance at a little action in the bedroom.

'Good. Then I guess I don't have to worry about you escaping,' Grace said then before stepping away from the bed and picking up my trousers. I watched her rummaging around in my pockets but had no idea why.

'What are you doing?'

'I'm getting your wallet.'

'Why?'

'Because I need your debit card.'

'What for?'

'I have a meal to pay for tonight. Now, if you will excuse me, I have a dinner date to make, and I don't want to be late for it. I'll be a little early, but I thought I'd have a few cocktails beforehand. Apparently, that French restaurant you booked has a lovely bar area, but I'll be the judge of that.'

That was when I realised what Grace was doing. She wasn't punishing me in the sense of some type of fun sex game. She was punishing me in the very literal sense of I had annoyed her by working today, so she was now going to leave me tied up in the hotel room while she went out and enjoyed our dinner reservation with my bank card.

‘Wait, you’re joking, right?’ I cried as I watched Grace head for the door while I wriggled my wrists and fought against my restraints.

‘Were you joking about leaving me all day to do some work?’ she snapped back, but we both knew the answer to that one, and before I could say anything more, the door was open, and my wife was leaving.

‘Now you will know how it feels to be left alone,’ she said before departing, and as the door closed behind her, I begged one more time.

‘Wait! Grace! Come back! You can’t leave me like this!’

But leave me she did.

18

DOMINIC

I've just finished telling Kamilla the story of the time Grace locked me up in a hotel room for over two hours while she went out and had dinner by herself, and as I expected, the reaction to the tale is not a positive one.

'You have to be joking? She actually did that?'

'Yes.'

'And you stayed with her?'

'I was upset and angry at the time, but I understood that Grace was too.'

'But that didn't give her the right to tie you to a bed and leave you!'

Kamilla is right. It was a terrible reaction by my wife to how I had treated her that day in Bath. Yes, I'd promised her a romantic weekend only to leave her while I went and dealt with work, but there was no need to handcuff me to a bed. Shout at me, sure. Call me a workaholic. Tell me you deserve to be treated a little better. But don't treat me like a damn prisoner. But that's what my wife did.

And now she has done it again.

'So what happened? She just came back from dinner, uncuffed you and said sorry?'

'Well, no, not exactly. She didn't apologise.'

'What?'

'She never said sorry. She just acted like everything was okay.'

'And you let her get away with it? You didn't tell her that she was crazy and that you might leave her?'

'No.'

'My God, how weak are you?'

'Hey!'

'No, I'm serious! It sounds like Grace gave you a pretty big warning four years ago, yet you ignored it. Even better, you thought it was a good idea to start having an affair, knowing full well that if your wife found out, she might not react in a healthy way!'

'How the hell was I to know she would lock us away if she caught us?'

'Because she locked you away once before! If you'd left her then, as you should have done, then we wouldn't be in this mess now!'

'Oh, come off it! You wouldn't have looked at me twice if I'd been single.'

'What are you talking about now?'

'I'm talking about the fact that you clearly have a thing for older, married men. Call it a fetish or whatever. But I know why you like me, and it's not just because I'm reasonably handsome for a guy my age. It's because I'm taken. You got a thrill from having another woman's man. So, if I hadn't been with Grace, this affair would never have happened. Therefore, me not leaving her after she tied me to that bed in Bath is irrelevant.'

Kamilla tries to deny it, but I just shake my head and toss the screwed-up note into the air a couple of times. I regret telling her about what happened in Bath now, but I regret not taking that incident more seriously at the time too. Kamilla is right. I should have reacted differently once Grace had returned to the hotel room and taken off the handcuffs. I should have been stronger. At least threatened to leave her. But maybe my other woman is right. Maybe I am weak.

'I'm sorry. Us fighting isn't going to help things,' Kamilla admits, and I'm at least glad she won't be having another go at me again. 'This is just bad luck. We couldn't have expected this to happen. Sure, people get caught having affairs all the time, but how many of them get locked in a cabin?'

'Some of them end up worse than this.'

'What?'

'I'm just saying, some people who get caught cheating don't just get locked up. They get murdered by the angry party. A crime of passion, I think they call it.'

'Why the hell would you say that?'

'I don't know. I'm just trying to look on the bright side.'

'There is no bright side! Just because we haven't been shot or stabbed, that doesn't mean we should be grateful! We've still been locked up by a crazy bitch!'

I've given up trying to defend Grace from being called things like that now and because I have, Kamilla continues to warm to her theme.

'After what you've just told me, it's obvious now that we are dealing with a seriously damaged person. If her reaction to being slighted is to restrain somebody and leave them helpless then clearly something very bad happened to her in her childhood.'

'I don't know about that.'

‘Think about it! It must have because people who have a normal upbringing don’t go around doing this to people. Once might be a bad reaction but twice? That’s a pattern of behaviour, and I want to know where the hell it stems from. Was she tied up as a child? Was that how her parents punished her when she was naughty? Or maybe she had a weird ex who did that to her? What I’m saying is, she must have learnt this from somewhere.’

‘I think you’re overthinking this.’

‘Am I? One of us has to because you’re clearly not doing any thinking!’

‘Are you kidding? I’m trying to think of ways to get us out of here. But I can’t concentrate if you’re going to keep throwing around all sorts of crazy theories.’

I want to leave it there, but Kamilla keeps going, referring to Grace’s past and whatever skeletons might be lurking there that we don’t know about.

‘Has she ever done this to anybody else? Has she ever mentioned locking other people away?’

‘What? No!’

‘Are you sure? Because if she has mentioned something, anything at all, it might help us.’

‘She hasn’t!’

‘I just find it hard to believe that this is the first time she has done this! Not with the way she is acting so cool about it!’

I’m unsettled by the thought that Grace might have done this to somebody else before, which is why I force it from my mind as quickly as I can.

I get up and go over to the window, not particularly interested in looking outside but needing to turn my back to Kamilla for a moment while I try and calm down. When I look through the glass, I see everything as it was before in the garden, which doesn't give my mood a reason to improve. And it only gets worse as Kamilla keeps throwing around ideas as to why Grace is the way she is.

'I bet somebody did this to her once. Maybe she was young; maybe she was older. But somebody had to have tied her up, probably when she had done something wrong, to teach her a lesson. And the experience must have taught her how powerless it feels to be left like this. So now she knows to use it on others, or at least you anyway.'

I say nothing as I grit my teeth and squeeze the ball of paper in my left hand, while staring at the kitchen door and wishing it would open.

'Can you imagine how scarred she might be from somebody doing this to her?' Kamilla muses. 'I'm not excusing it, no way, but something has clearly damaged her, and she needs professional help. Before she goes too far and kills somebody.'

'She's not going to kill anybody. She let me out that day in the hotel, and she'll let us out now. She just needs time.'

'How much? A day? A week? A month? Until we're both wasting away, and she looks through the windows at our dehydrated, starved bodies and realises she better open the door before we die a horrible death?'

God, I wish I had some way of shutting Kamilla up. Nothing too forceful. Just an off-switch on her that I could press so she would stop talking for one goddamn minute and give me time to think. But humans aren't wired like that. There's no off-switch. Everyone has their own tendencies. Grace does, and Kamilla does. I'm just the one suffering the brunt of them.

'I'm going to write her a note,' Kamilla says suddenly, getting up off the floor and going over to my desk, where she picks up a piece of paper and starts hunting around for something to write with. The pencil is on my desk somewhere, but she hasn't found it yet. But before she does, I say something else I end up regretting.

'Don't bother. It won't work.'

'How do you know? It might do. I'll write something saying that I understand if she was treated badly in the past, and this is the only way she knows to lash out. It's a cry for help. Whatever. I'll be nice. Offer sympathy. It might work.'

'No, it won't.'

'At least I'm trying something. You're just being useless!'

'I already tried it!'

So much for keeping my note a secret. In a desperate bid to prove that I'm not actually useless, I have confessed to writing the note. The one that I'm still holding in my hand.

'What? You wrote her a note? When?'

'While you were asleep?'

'What did it say?'

'It doesn't matter.'

'Of course it matters! You're not the only one locked up in here! I'm in this too, so I have a right to know!'

I say nothing, but Kamilla looks at the paper ball that I'm still holding tightly, and she figures it out.

'Is that it? Is that the note you wrote? Is that why you wanted it? You didn't want me to read it, did you? What does it say?'

'I told you, it doesn't matter. It didn't work. That's all you need to know.'

'Just give me it. I want to read it.'

'No.'

'Dom! Stop acting like we're against each other. We're on the same team here!'

Kamilla is right, so I eventually concede and toss her the paper.

'Fine, read it. But I already told you it didn't work, so you're just wasting your time.'

Kamilla catches the paper ball and opens it up quickly, tearing it a little in her haste before she starts reading. I let out a deep sigh and go back to staring out of the window helplessly until she has finished with it, and once she has, she has more things to say.

'Wow, you really did grovel to her, didn't you?'

'I wrote what I could to try and get us out of here.'

'Yeah, I can see that. It was a nice try. But what's this at the bottom? *You men are all the same.*'

'That's what she wrote back.'

'Grace wrote that?'

'Yeah, after I'd pushed the note under the door. She sent it back with that on it.'

'Why would she say that?'

'I don't know. Isn't it just a thing all women say about men who have done wrong? *They're all the same.*'

'In a jokey situation, maybe. But not one like this. For her to have written that, she must really mean it.'

'Well, I guess she does then.'

'But if so, she must be going on experience. Another man in her past must have cheated on her. An ex, perhaps.'

'I don't know, maybe. She never mentioned anything like that to me.'

'Are you sure?'

'Yeah. What does it matter? It doesn't help us anyway!'

'I'm just trying to understand her. I told you that! If we can understand her, we might be able to figure out exactly what we need to do to get her to open this door.'

'There is no understanding her! I've told you! I've been married to her all this time, and I'm only just realising now that I never knew her. So if I don't know her then good luck to you figuring her out in the next few hours!'

I punch the wooden wall beside me, my anger getting the better of me, and the noise is so loud that Kamilla is startled. My hand is hurt from the action, and I hold it gingerly, wishing I hadn't done that and now worried that I might have a broken bone to add to my list of woes.

I slump down to the floor again while clutching my wounded hand, and as Kamilla looks down at me with an expression that can only be described as like looking at a sick puppy who probably just needs putting out of its misery, I shake my head and repeat my last point.

'I don't know Grace. I don't know what makes her tick. I wish I did, but I'm clearly out of my depth here. And you can bet that she knows it.'

19

GRACE

Work goes surprisingly quickly when you're in a good mood. Despite having several tedious tasks on my To-Do list, ranging from sending emails to reading reports, I am feeling quite chipper, and that's because I keep thinking about Dominic and that woman suffering in the cabin.

They must be so hungry now, not to mention exhausted. And I bet they would both give anything to be able to put some clothes on. Yes, I'm quite enjoying thinking about the pair of naked cheats going through a tough time as I sit here at my desk with the key to the cabin in my handbag.

I'm so calm and collected that I didn't miss a beat when a few of my colleagues asked me why I left the event early last night instead of staying on as originally planned. It was easy to just tell them that I was tired and preferred to have my own bed rather than a hotel one, and they accepted that answer before filling me in on any gossip I might have missed after I'd departed.

We were halfway through all that gossip when we learnt one of our colleagues who hadn't been at the event last night had baked a cake and had brought it into the office today for us all to have a piece at lunch. I have to say that I did enjoy my slice of cake when it was served to me during our break, and I thanked the baker as I nibbled on my piece and got crumbs all over myself. Somebody asked me if I liked to bake cakes, and when I said sometimes, they hinted that I should bake one this weekend, so I could bring it in on Monday and cheer us all up on that most awful of days. But I declined because somehow, I think I'll be busy enough with other things this weekend.

I still haven't decided when exactly I'm going to unlock that cabin door and let Dominic and *her* out. Before I do that, I need to make a plan for damage limitation. They'll be angry, so I need to fan those flames of rage before I open the door, and my best way of doing that might be the same way Dominic tried to calm me down.

His note under the door was a good ploy, I'll give him that, and it'll probably be the best way for me to correspond with him as well. I wasn't ready to write anything too deep and meaningful earlier, limiting myself to a short retort at the end of his note, but perhaps I'll have a go at reaching out to him with a lengthier message later tonight once my working day is done, and I'm back home again. But before that can happen, I have one obstacle to overcome, and it comes in the form of the invitation I receive to go for after-work drinks with a few of the other women in my office.

'Come on, we've all been talking about trying that new bar around the corner. Well, tonight is the night! Let's do it!'

That was the rallying cry from Tina, the woman sitting two desks over from me and the one who is always the instigator of any social events in this workplace. Normally, I'd be thrilled to go out for a few drinks with the people I work with because I don't have too many friends, and it's nice to be included. But tonight, I just want to get back to my house so that I can check on the couple in the cabin. Coming to the office today was a necessity because I have to earn a living, but going out for cocktails would be a frivolous use of my time when something so important is going on in my personal life. So that's why I politely decline the invitation and promise Tina that I will make the next trip and that she will have to tell me all about how it went at the new bar when I see her on Monday.

Tina isn't quite as disappointed at me saying no as I might have hoped she would be. That goes for the rest of my colleagues too. I'd have quite liked it if they begged me to change my mind and at least pretended like they would miss me not being there. I'm not exactly the life and soul of any party but still, it would be nice to be missed. As it is, the colleagues who are going are quickly over the disappointment of those who aren't and spend the rest of the afternoon chattering excitedly about their upcoming evening and just how tipsy they all might be by the end of the night.

I stay mostly quiet for the rest of the day, silently ticking off my list of assignments until the clock hits five and I can finally get out of here. Then, as my co-workers file out of the office in search of their first proper drink of the day, I make my way across the car park to Dominic's vehicle, leaving my own car in the car park again because I can get away with it being here, before getting behind the wheel, turning on the radio and setting off in the direction of home.

Singing away to the song playing on my favourite radio station, my good mood lasts all the way until I reach the Chinese takeaway about ten minutes from my house. I go inside and order my usual, and by usual, I mean an obscene amount of food. A smorgasbord of sweet and sour chicken, egg fried rice, prawn crackers, not to mention a couple of other sides that my waistline doesn't need but my ravenous appetite certainly does.

It's while I'm in the takeaway waiting for my food to cook that I think about Dominic and what he would order. He's a beef and black bean man, and he loves it whenever I suggest we treat ourselves to a Chinese, but there'll be no tasty food for him tonight. The best he'll get is the hint of a smell of my food if it wafts out from inside the house and drifts down towards the bottom of the garden, but if that happens, it will only serve him right for what he has done. I'm sure he'll regret his actions even more if he knows I'm tucking into a tasty meal while his stomach growls and desperately tries to consume whatever bit of food might be leftover from the last thing he ate yesterday.

What about his woman in the cabin with him? Does she like Chinese food? Or is it too unhealthy for her? Is she more of a salad and a fruit smoothie type of girl? Potentially, considering how much slimmer she is than me. But she'll soon be regretting not having a few more fat reserves to draw upon as her own hunger grows by the hour.

Serves her right, the skinny bitch.

I thank the man who hands me my large, overpacked plastic bag full of hot food containers before I leave the takeaway and return to my car to complete my journey home. The music on the radio is not quite as good as it was earlier, but I still find a couple of tracks to sing along to, and by the time I park on my driveway, I am feeling good. That mood only continues as I get inside the house and dish up my delicious meal onto a large plate while glancing out of the kitchen window at the cabin and seeing that the door is still very much closed, as it should be.

The thought occurs to me that I could go down to the cabin window and show my food to the people inside, but that seems a little too cruel, even for me, so I don't do that. But I do make sure to open the kitchen window, so they might pick up a few smells before I tuck into my meal, chewing it down hungrily and feeding my enormous appetite.

It's not long until I experience the usual post-meal feelings of guilt at consuming so many calories, but better to feel guilty about food than what I'm currently doing to my cheating husband and his mistress, and as I put my dirty plate into the dishwasher and throw away the empty containers, I think about how guilt is such a strange emotion. Sometimes it comes, sometimes it doesn't, even when a person is thinking about the same thing. I don't feel guilty about what I've done to Dominic and that woman today, yet I definitely felt guilty the last time I locked two people away.

The memory of that guilt comes to me now, washing over me almost as quickly as the water in this machine will be washing over my dirty plate once I've put the cleaning tablet inside and turned it on. I felt so guilty after what I did to Dad all those years ago, not that anybody knew it at the time. That was because, just like today, I was very good at keeping quiet.

20

GRACE

TEN YEARS OLD

The police are at my house. They came after Mum called them. I heard her on the phone to them half an hour ago from my hiding place at the top of the stairs.

Mum thought I was asleep in bed, but I was awake, listening to everything that was going on, and that's how I knew she called the police and told them about Dad being missing. Now there are two police officers in my house, although I'm not currently creeping at the top of the stairs anymore. I'm back in bed with the duvet pulled tightly over my head, and I plan on staying here until the police have left. That's because I'm scared that they might try and speak to me, and if they do, this might be when all the trouble starts.

I saw Mum open the door, and a man and woman came into the house, both wearing scary-looking uniforms like I have seen the police wear on TV. My heart was beating very fast when I saw them, and I got scared they would see me too, so I sneaked back into my bedroom, afraid to listen to what they might be saying to Mum in case they were talking about me. But it's been a while now, and I don't know what's going on down there.

All I know is that the police are still here.

And Dad is still missing.

I've missed my chance. I should have told Mum what I did to Dad before she phoned the police. Now it's too late. If I tell her now with them here then they might arrest me, and I'll go to prison. I don't want that. Prison is bad. I know about it because someone in my class has a parent in prison. Other kids tease them about it, saying they are going to be a criminal too, just like their dad and that they'll end up locked away in a tiny room with no food and water, left and forgotten, with nobody coming to visit them.

What if that happens to me? What if I'm locked away and forgotten about? Mum and Dad wouldn't visit me, would they? They would be too angry at me. And nobody else would come because I don't have anybody else. No one from school would come to see me. I would be all alone. *Forever.*

So I won't say anything now.

No way.

I suddenly hear footsteps coming up the stairs, and my heart starts beating fast again because I worry it's the police coming to get me. What should I say to them if it is? Should I try and pretend I've done nothing wrong, like I used to when I was younger and got in trouble with Mum and Dad? Or should I just admit what I did and beg for forgiveness, like I sometimes did when I knew Mum and Dad knew what I'd done, so there was no point even trying to deny it?

I don't know.

So I just pull my duvet over my head a little more.

I hear the footsteps getting nearer, and I'm just waiting for the light from the hallway to start shining through my duvet to let me know that my bedroom door is now open, and somebody is looking in at me. But that doesn't happen. There is no light because the footsteps move past my room and carry on down the hallway before I hear somebody close and lock the bathroom door.

They haven't come for me yet.

I'm still free.

Gaining a little confidence, I peep out over the edge of my duvet, looking across my dark room at the door that remains shut. All is quiet. Have the police gone? Was that Mum coming up to bed?

I have to know, so I creep out of bed and go to my door, opening it slightly and looking out. The lights in the hallway are still on, but there is nobody around. I can't hear any voices downstairs either. Maybe the police have left. Maybe I am not in trouble after all.

I suddenly hear the toilet flush. Mum must be about to come out of the bathroom. I better get back into bed in case she sees me. But I also want to know what happened with the police. What did she tell them? And what did they say?

I wait for the bathroom door to open, and it takes a while, but it eventually does. I open my own door a little more, ready to appear so I can talk to Mum. But at the last second, I see that it isn't her. There's a uniform. It's a police officer. The woman, not the man. They are still here.

And now they have seen me.

'Oh, hello. I'm sorry. Did I wake you?'

The policewoman smiles at me, which makes me think I might not be in trouble because if I was, why would she be nice to me?

'No, I was already awake,' I tell her before wishing that I hadn't because I don't want Mum knowing I haven't been asleep all this time.

'I'm just here to talk to your Mum. She's downstairs. Everything's okay, you don't need to worry,' she tells me, but I'm not sure why because everything is not okay, is it?

Unless they've found Dad, and he hasn't told them what I did.

'What's happening?' I ask, still clutching the side of my bedroom door, not wanting to commit to fully leaving my room. In this position, I still feel like I have a chance of running back to my bed before the policewoman can get me. So I won't get any nearer to her, and I won't let her get any nearer to me.

The policewoman doesn't answer my question though, not telling me what is happening, even though I know why she is here. Then we both hear movement downstairs.

'Grace. What are you doing out of bed?'

I look down to see Mum standing on the stairs looking up at me. I've been caught.

'It's not her fault. I think I might have woken her when I went to the bathroom,' the policewoman says. 'I'm sorry.'

'You should be fast asleep now, young girl,' Mum tells me, but I just ask her what is going on.

'It's about your father,' Mum replies before telling me to get back into bed. But I don't do that. I just keep asking more questions, wanting to know the answers rather than spend any more time worrying under my duvet.

Mum keeps urging me to go back to bed, but I keep refusing, telling her I can't sleep until she concedes and allows me to come downstairs, and as the three of us go into the living room, I see the policeman sitting in there writing something on a notepad.

I feel confident that they aren't going to arrest me, so I'm happy now to sit with them and listen to what is happening, and as I do, I hear all sorts of things.

'Like we said, it's still early. I know it's easy to say, but I would try not to worry yet.'

'Most things like this are resolved in the first twenty-four hours.'

'We'll start looking, though, and let you know as soon as we find him.'

'Try and get some sleep. I'm sure everything will be okay.'

The police officers said all of that in between Mum saying some things of her own.

'I just don't understand why he wouldn't call.'

'He's never done anything like this before.'

'Something is wrong. I can just feel it.'

'What if I haven't heard anything by the morning?'

I'm the only one who doesn't say anything. I just sit there quietly on the edge of the sofa, staring at my feet and thinking about how all of this is happening because of me. It sounds like they still don't know where Dad is. That means they don't know I'm the one who locked him away yet. But it also means he is still there in that shed with that woman.

What should I do?

A quick look up at the police uniforms reminds me that telling the truth now will be a very scary thing to do. So I keep quiet again until the police officers stand up to leave, and they both smile at me before they walk out of the room with Mum following behind them, still asking them a lot of questions.

I feel better once they have gone, and it's just me and Mum in the house again. But for how long? The police said they would be back in the morning. Hopefully, I'll be at school by then, and I won't have to see them. That will be easier than this.

'You need to get in bed. Now.'

Mum's voice is stern, and I know not to disagree with her when she sounds like this, so I just nod my head and go to do as she says. But just before I leave the room, I hear something. When I turn back, I see that Mum is crying.

'Are you okay?' I ask her, and she tells me that she is before she starts crying harder, reaching for a box of tissues as tears run down her cheeks.

I've never seen Mum cry before. I'm always the one crying in front of her. I don't like seeing it. I wish I could make the tears stop.

'Mum…'

I go to tell her what I've done. Where Dad is. Why I locked him away.

She stops crying as she looks at me, ready to hear what I have to say.

That was the moment. The moment I should have just told the truth. It could have all ended there, and everything would have been so different, for me, for Mum, and for Dad. For the rest of our lives. But I didn't know that then. I just got scared and stopped talking.

Then I went back to bed.

I left Mum crying downstairs.

21

GRACE

I turned the power back on in the cabin ten minutes ago. I'm not sure why. Maybe it was because I felt a little sorry for them. Or maybe it's because I've been thinking about Mum and Dad, and that has given me a reason to slightly reconsider being so cruel to my husband and his other woman. But that's all I've done. I've not visited the cabin, I've not given those inside an opportunity to talk to me, and I've certainly not unlocked that door yet.

It's eight o'clock on a Friday night, and I'm all alone, nothing for company but a bad television programme and a solitary glass of wine. Is this how life has to be for me now? Maybe so, unless I forgive Dominic for what he's done. Or I could find somebody new to take his place.

One thing at a time.

I need to figure out what to do with my current husband before I entertain any thoughts about the next one.

The sound of the doorbell almost causes me to drop my glass of wine because I'm not expecting company. But somebody has come to visit, and I have no idea who it is as I leave the living room and tentatively approach the door.

Is it someone I know? Is it someone looking for that woman in the cabin? *Or is it the police?*

It turns out its just my neighbour, Maggie. She has a big smile on her face and a bottle of wine in her hand, and when I ask her if everything is okay, she tells me that she has called around because Frank told her I was going to be home alone this weekend.

That's right, I told Frank that Dominic was going to be working away. The lie helped me out at the time. But it's just given me another problem now. While it's nice of Maggie to check on me while I'm alone, I'm not actually alone at all, and the last thing I need is her coming inside and figuring that out.

'Oh, that's very kind of you,' I say, forcing a smile onto my own face. 'But I'm absolutely fine. You didn't have to worry about me.'

'Don't be silly, I'm not worried. You're a big girl, and I'm sure you can entertain yourself. If I'm honest, I just needed an excuse to get away from Frank for a couple of hours. So you'd actually be doing me the favour if you let me in for a glass of wine. So, how about it?'

Maggie waves the bottle in front of me, and I'm not sure what excuse I could give her to not let her in. It would just be plain rude of me to turn her away now, so very reluctantly, I step aside and welcome her inside.

It'll be okay. We'll just stay in the house. We won't go in the garden, so there's no way she'll see or hear anything at the cabin. And I'll try and keep her away from the windows so she can't look out, but even if she does, it's going dark now, so the failing light will keep my secrets hidden in the shadows.

'How about I open this and you take a seat in the living room?' I suggest to Maggie as I take the bottle from her and guide her to the sofa because that way, she won't follow me into the kitchen and look into the back garden.

'Sounds good to me, neighbour.'

I serve up the drinks and turn off the TV, making a quick joke about what I'd been watching before Maggie showed up here unannounced, before we go through the fairly mundane beginnings of small talk.

Maggie asks me about how my day has been, how work is and how I am in general, and I do a good job of giving her very normal, safe answers, not hinting at all that my life has actually been turned upside down, and I still don't know when it will be corrected again.

'What about you?' I ask her, turning it back on to her. 'Everything good?'

I'm not expecting Maggie to launch into a list of problems that she might have, but that ends up being exactly what happens, and the more she talks, the more it becomes apparent she really did mean it when she said she wanted to get away from her husband for a couple of hours tonight.

'Can I be honest?' Maggie asks me, and I say yes because rather her than me. 'I think I've just got a little bored of Frank. Is that a bad thing to say?'

'Oh, erm, bad? No. Surprising, maybe.'

'I'm sorry. I shouldn't have said anything.'

'No, it's okay. Go on.'

If anything, I'm actually quite welcoming this distraction from my own problems.

'It's just that we've been married for twenty years now, and things have got, how can I say it? A little stale.'

'In the bedroom?'

'Everywhere.'

'Oh, okay.'

'He doesn't surprise me anymore. He barely even talks to me. He just takes me for granted. And I guess I treat him the same way. We're both just coasting, and I'm not sure what I want to do about that. I'm not sure I even care anymore.'

'I don't know what to say.'

'Tell me I'm mad. Tell me it'll be okay. Tell me how you and Dominic are so happy together.'

I could have laughed at that last sentence if things weren't so bleak in reality, but I manage to keep my composure.

'I wouldn't say we're perfect. No couple is. Everyone has their problems.'

'But that's my point. We don't have a problem, per se. Everything is fine. Neither one of us has strayed. Neither one of us has got violent or started acting unfairly to the other one. Maybe if any of those things had happened then it would make it easier.'

'Trust me, you don't want to wish for one of you to cheat,' I say sadly.

'Oh, really? You sound like you're speaking from experience.'

Maggie is looking at me like she hopes I'll elaborate on my point but, of course, I don't.

'No, I don't have any experience with that kind of thing at all, thank God,' I say, dismissing the notion. 'I'm just saying. Be grateful you don't have a problem like that.'

'I suppose. But what am I supposed to do? Just carry on in a stale relationship for the next twenty years? Or do something about it?'

'I don't know. Maybe you should talk to Frank.'

'I've tried. He just shrugs and says we're fine. Then he goes back to watching sport and drinking beer. Do you know what he said to me the other day? He said he wished he had a cabin in the garden, like Dominic has. He didn't say why, but I got the hint. It's because he wishes he had somewhere he could go to get away from me in the evenings.'

The mention of the cabin makes me think of my husband and that woman out there now, a little warmer inside the cabin now that the power is back on but still very much under my control.

'Do you think that's why Dominic wanted his cabin?' Maggie asks me. 'To have some peace and privacy.'

'No, it's just a place he can work when he's not at the office.'

'But he's in there a lot, right?'

A lot more than you realise, my dear neighbour.

'I guess.'

'Do you think it's helped you two? Him having somewhere to go? Gives you both some space every now and then?'

'I don't know.'

It's certainly helped me lock him up, that's for sure.

'I guess what I'm getting at is do you think I should let Frank build a cabin in the garden?'

I feel like telling her no because she has no idea the problems it can cause. But I can't give anything away, so I just shrug and tell her it might not be a bad idea.

'Maybe you can give me the details of the guys who built it for you,' Maggie suggests, and I say that will be fine before she picks up the wine bottle and pours herself another glass. I guess she isn't going anywhere yet.

But despite how awkward this conversation is for me, not to mention how unsettling it is to have somebody here while my husband is under lock and key only yards away from where we sit, I am actually quite glad to have Maggie here. It's nice to have another woman to talk to. I could have had that this evening if I'd gone for drinks with the women at work, but I didn't. But I've got company now, and it's clear that Maggie sees me as a friend if she is willing to confide in me about her problems at home.

A friend.

I remember those. They've been few and far between, but I have had some over the years.

I remember one friend in particular. She was the same age as me when we met under very unusual and very difficult circumstances. Her name was Rosie, and like me, she was sad on the day our paths crossed for the first time.

Rosie was my friend when I was ten years old.

But she would have hated me if she'd only known the truth about me at the time.

22

GRACE

TEN YEARS OLD

The police are no longer just looking for one missing person.

They're now looking for two.

The woman who is with Dad has also been reported as missing, and a policeman has just finished telling Mum who she is.

'Her name is Amy, and her husband reported her missing not long after you spoke to us about your own husband,' the policeman says, and I know that because I've snuck downstairs and am currently eavesdropping on the conversation going on on the other side of the living room door.

'What has this got to do with my husband?' Mum asks, still oblivious to the fact I'm not in bed, which I'm glad about because she would not react well if she knew I was sneaking around the house while the police were here.

'I mention it because it's unusual for two people of a similar age to go missing at the same time in the same place, especially in this town.'

'So what are you saying?' Mum asks. 'You think it might be linked?'

'It's a possibility.'

'How?'

'We don't know. It could just be a coincidence, of course, but we have to consider everything.'

'And what's everything?'

There is a pause in the conversation then before the policeman goes on.

'It's possible that your husband and this other woman, Amy, may have known each other and if so, they may be together.'

Another pause. Mum isn't saying anything. What is she thinking? I wish I could see her, but I dare not peep around this half-open door in case she spots me.

'What do you mean, *together*?'

Mum has found her voice again.

'I'm just saying they could be connected. But it's too early to know for sure yet.'

'Are you saying my husband was having an affair?'

'No, not at all!'

'Then what are you saying?'

Mum is getting cross, and I feel bad for the policeman because it's no fun when Mum raises her voice.

'We're just trying to explore all possibilities. That means we need to consider if the two missing parties knew each other and may be together now. If so, then they may not be missing for a sinister reason.'

'What other reason is there for them both to disappear?'

Another pause, so Mum asks him again until he answers.

'They might have gone somewhere together.'

‘What do you mean? Like a hotel or something?’

‘I don’t know.’

‘No, I think you are hinting at something, so I’d appreciate it if you would have the balls to actually just man up and say it. You think they have run away together, my husband and this woman? Well, I’m not having it. He has a daughter, for God’s sake. He wouldn’t just leave her, never mind leave me as well!’

‘I understand. Like I said, we’ll keep you updated when we have some news.’

I think the policeman might be getting ready to leave now, so I scamper back up the stairs, careful not to make a sound but moving quickly so I’m out of the way before they come into the hallway.

I’ve made it back to the top of the stairs when I hear them talking by the front door. Mum is telling the policeman to try harder to get some concrete answers instead of just wild theories, and he is promising her that he and the other police officers will. Then he leaves, and Mum slams the door behind him, the noise loud enough to make me jump and probably the poor policeman out on the doorstep too.

I sneak back into bed and try and get some sleep, but all I can think about is how this is getting worse. I’m in so much trouble now. It’s not just Mum who is looking for somebody, but that other man is looking for his wife. Why did Dad and her have to do what they did? They are both married. They shouldn’t have been together, kissing each other in that shed. It should have been empty. I should have just been able to hide there then go home, and everything would have been okay. But now it's all ruined.

Another day goes by, but nothing much happens. I thought about going back to the shed, but it was raining, and I got scared that somebody might see me and know it was me who locked it, so I stayed away. Then I have another night without sleep, but I know Mum hasn't been sleeping either because she keeps yawning and telling her friend on the phone that the only thing keeping her going at the moment is coffee.

I also hear her say something else to her friend. She says that Dad always had a wandering eye and that maybe this time, he actually did more than just look. I don't really know what that means, but she says it a few times before she starts crying again, and then she gets angry, calling Dad a liar and saying that if he has been having an affair then he better not come home because she will kill him if he does.

It's the next day when the police return to our house and when they do, I'm asked to be in the room with Mum. I don't know why they want me now, but I think it can't be good, but Mum doesn't say anything as I sit on the sofa next to her. She just takes a sip of her drink. But it's not coffee anymore. It's that red stuff that comes in the big bottles.

'I'm afraid we still have no news,' a man in a dark suit tells us. I wonder why he isn't wearing a uniform like the other police officers. Maybe he is more important than them. Or maybe it's a non-uniform day for him like I sometimes get to have at school.

‘As it’s now been four days since the missing person’s report was filed, we need to try something else. I am going to make an appeal to the public for information, and I was hoping you would be willing to speak alongside me at that appeal.’

Mum’s fingernails tap the edge of her glass loudly before she has another drink, and then she asks what she would have to say at the appeal.

‘Just say whatever you want to. How you feel. You miss your husband. You want to know if he is safe. You want him to come home. Anything like that. Just be honest.’

‘Why should I?’

‘Excuse me?’

‘Why should I be honest? My husband clearly hasn’t been honest with me. He’s ran off with this woman and left me looking like a fool.’

The man in the suit looks a bit awkward, and I see him look at one of the police officers before he speaks again.

‘I understand that this is a difficult time for you, and you have all sorts of concerns. But as I told you earlier, there has been no activity on your husband’s bank accounts or any activity at all that might suggest he has gone to start a new life elsewhere.’

‘He’s with her. This woman. *Amy*. He has to be.’

‘Maybe. But there has been no activity on her bank accounts, nor did either of them withdraw any substantial amounts of money prior to their disappearances. To me, that doesn’t fit the profile of two people trying to run away. They’d need money, wherever they have gone, and as far as we can tell, they don't have that. Nor have they been detected on CCTV in the area. It's as if they have both just vanished, but people don't just vanish, not in this day and age. They leave tracks. The fact there are no tracks here is leading me to think something has happened to them.'

Mum doesn't say anything to that. She just finishes her drink and goes to pick up the bottle on the table beside the sofa. But the man in the suit speaks again before she can pour another glass.

'The appeal will be tomorrow morning. It would be best if you had a good night's rest before it.'

But Mum just laughs at that before pouring herself another drink and taking an even bigger sip than the last one.

'Okay, fine. I'll speak at the appeal,' she says with a shrug. 'But I'll be damned if you're going to come into my house and suggest that I should stop drinking. Now, if you don't mind and if you don't have anything else to tell me, leave me and my daughter alone.'

I stay sitting with Mum while everybody else leaves, but when they're all gone, she just tells me to go to bed. I say that I want to stay up with her and try to give her a hug, but she just shouts at me to do as I'm told, and I end up running from the room as she raises her voice before I hear the sound of glass smashing against a wall.

Mum didn't come to bed that night. I find her asleep on the sofa when I come downstairs in the morning. There is also a big red patch on the wall behind the TV, as well as some pieces of glass on the carpet. But we don't have time to tidy up because the police come to get us for the appeal.

After a drive in the car, we arrive at some big building across town. There are a lot of people in the room we are taken into. Some of them have police uniforms on but others don't, and I'm not sure who they are. But they are all rushing around and talking to people with cameras, and I can also see somebody setting up microphones on a big table at the front of the room.

There are lots of seats near the table, and while the police speak to Mum, the chairs fill up with men and women who have tape recorders and notepads and who seem to be typing a lot of messages on their mobile phones as they wait for something to happen. But in amongst the crowded room, I see a little girl who looks to be my age. She is wearing a white dress, and she is holding the hand of a teenage boy in a white shirt. I guess it's her brother because she looks a bit like him. Then I notice that she is looking right at me.

She gives me a wave.

So I wave back.

I don't go and talk to her because I know to stay near Mum, but when the time comes for Mum to go to the big table at the front, I am told to go into a small room nearby to wait for her. In there, I see the little girl and her brother again, and with all the adults in the room watching the TV screens that are showing what is happening in the other room, I am free to talk to the girl.

'What's your name?' I ask her quietly.

'Rosie. What's yours?'

'Grace.'

'How old are you?'

'Ten.'

'Me too.'

'Is that your brother?'

'Yeah, Joshua. He's thirteen.'

I smile at the older boy, but he doesn't smile back.

'Why are you here?' Rosie asks me then.

'My mum is making an appeal. Why are you here?'

'My dad is making an appeal too.'

Joshua tells me their mum is missing, and I guess she is Amy, the woman who is with Dad in the shed. But I don't say anything because the appeal starts then, and suddenly, Mum's face is on the TV screens in the room.

It's weird seeing her on TV, but kind of cool as well, and I watch her as she talks, asking for any news on where Dad might be before she starts crying and has to stop. Then it's time for Amy's husband to talk, and he asks for the same thing before he ends up crying even more than Mum did. Then the man in the suit appears, and he says some things, but I miss all of it because Rosie asks me if I want to say a prayer for our missing parents. I don't really know what to do because I never do this kind of thing, but she holds my hand and says a few things before she smiles at me.

'They'll be okay,' she tells me. 'They'll be home soon.'

I like Rosie. She is nice. But she is also wrong. My dad and her mum won't be home soon unless I go and let them out of that shed. But after meeting Rosie and feeling like I want to be her friend, I make a decision.

I am going to go to that shed as soon as I can and open the door.

It's time to let them out.

It's time for everybody to stop worrying. Mum. Rosie. Joshua. Me.

It's time for this to be over.

23

GRACE

With my history, it's probably no surprise that I've found relationships difficult. Trust issues. Paranoia. Guilt. None of those things generally contribute to a person who will find it easy to make friends and keep them. But Maggie is still here now, in my house, and chatting away to me as if we're besties. Now she is on to telling me about how she recently found out that her husband follows all sorts of scantily-clad celebrities on his social media accounts.

'I had wondered why he had an account on some of those websites,' Maggie says. 'He told me he liked to follow some famous sportsmen. Golfers and people like that. Said it could teach him a few things for his own swing. But when I looked at the accounts he followed, there were a few golfers, but they were greatly outnumbered by lingerie models.'

I almost laugh at that because the thought of Frank ogling some model half his age, via his mobile phone and all while he assumes his wife thinks he is watching tips on how to be a better golfer, is amusing to me. But I manage to keep it in because Maggie doesn't seem to think it's very funny herself.

'How would he like it if I started following a load of accounts for shirtless men? I bet he'd get jealous, wouldn't he?' Maggie asks.

'Probably.'

'So why is it one rule for him and one for me?'

'Have you spoken to him about this?'

'No.'

'Maybe do that. Give him a chance to explain himself.'

I was only saying something that I thought might be able to help Maggie feel better about this, but no sooner have the words left my mouth then I realise that I am not following the advice I have just dished out. I haven't given Dominic his chance to explain himself yet. Nor have I offered that opportunity to the woman he is locked away with.

Is that fair?

Maggie is whittering on about something else Frank has done to annoy her lately, but now all my thoughts are about getting her out of my house as quickly as possible so I can go out to the garden and communicate with those in the cabin. I start to fake a few yawns and steal a couple of glances over at the clock on the mantelpiece, and though it takes a while, Maggie eventually starts to get the hint.

'Oh, I'm sorry. It's getting late, and you must be tired after a long week of work. I'll just finish this glass, and I'll get going.'

I pretend like it's okay, but a couple more stifled yawns, and Maggie has downed the remains of her wine and stood up to leave. But before I can get her out of the front door, she thanks me for acting as a sounding board for her this evening.

'I'm sorry if I unloaded all my problems with Frank onto you,' she says, looking only slightly remorseful about that. 'You're such a good listener. I hope Dominic appreciates you.'

I can't contain my laughter this time, and Maggie looks confused.

'What's funny?'

'Oh, it's nothing. Sorry, I just get the giggles after wine sometimes.'

It's a lame lie, but Maggie buys it, and as I wave her off, I am still amused by how she said she hopes that my husband appreciates me.

With my neighbour gone, I quickly tidy up the empty glasses and bottle before finding a piece of paper and a pen and writing out a note to my prisoners.

It's been a while now since I caught you both in the act. I hope you understand how traumatic it was for me, and while locking you away all this time might seem like an overreaction, try and see it from my point of view. The pair of you have broken my heart. You're probably wondering how long it will be until I let you out, but I'm wondering how long it will be until my heart is mended again.

In the meantime, I'll give you a chance to explain yourselves. I want each of you to tell me why you did what you did. Dominic, be honest. Was it for the cheap thrill? Was it just pure lust? Or have you gotten bored of me and needed some excitement in your life? And you, my love rival, why did you decide to sleep with an older, married man? A fantasy? A fetish? Or can you not get somebody your own age? I'd like the answers to these questions in written form and be prompt, it's getting late, and I'm tired. Depending on

how honest you are with me will determine if the cabin door is unlocked tonight.

Satisfied with the note, I deliver it to the cabin, sliding it under the door before waiting for it to come back with some answers written on it. I put my coat on just before I left the house, so I'm not too chilly, plus the glass of wine I had with Maggie is helping take the edge off. But I don't want to be lingering out here for too long, and I'm hoping that the urgency I tried to instil in my message is acted upon by the people reading it right now.

Rather predictably, Dominic and the woman appear at the cabin window quickly and try to communicate with me verbally through the glass. But I told them what I wanted, and it certainly wasn't them shouting at me and banging on the glass. They are to write back to me, and while they waste a couple of minutes ignoring that request, they eventually stop wasting all of our time and start putting pen to paper on their responses.

I can see the silhouettes of the two of them inside the gloomy cabin. They're both hunched over the desk beside the lamp, presumably working on what they are writing, and I see Dominic turn his head to look at me a couple of times before they are eventually done. Then the paper comes under the door, and I scoop it up quickly.

She has written first. I notice that her handwriting is pretty. Just like her.

I'm sorry for what I have done. I should never have gotten involved with a married man. To answer

your question as to why I did, I can only say that I am young and foolish, and like many other things I have done in my life, I've made mistakes and regret things, but I am striving to be better. I can only say sorry again.

It's a decent attempt, but I'm not having it that she is just blaming what she has done on being young and foolish, so I shake my head before going on to read what my husband has written.

Grace, like I said, I'm so sorry for hurting you. I can assure you that I have not gotten bored of you, nor was I seeking a cheap thrill. It just happened, unexpectedly and regretfully. But it means nothing. You are the only woman who means something to me.

I yawn again, but this time it is not a fake one. I am genuinely tired. Tired of reading this rubbish.

How long has it been going on?

That's my next question, and it goes under the door, leaving me to wait for the answer. I won't know for sure if they are lying or telling the truth, but I have to assume this isn't the first time they have been physical together. Their lovemaking probably started in hotel rooms before it progressed to my house, but I'll let them decide what they want to tell me.

The note comes back, and I see it is Dominic's handwriting that has been added to it. He's bravely fielding this question. Good for him.

Not long. A couple of weeks. I'm sorry.

Is he telling me the truth? I have no idea. But I do know that he is in danger of breaking the world record for the most number of times a person has said sorry in a twenty-four-hour period.

I wonder if he will use the ‘S’ word to answer my next question. It would be easy for him to do so, but I hope he takes the time to think a little more before giving his answer because this will be the most important question I ever ask of him and his partner in there.

It will also be the last one.

I write the question before taking a deep breath and thinking about whether or not I really want them to answer it well. If they do, they just might get out of this situation. But if they don’t, their torment will go on.

Let’s see what they can come up with. It’s not for me to decide what happens to them. They got themselves into this mess, and only they can get themselves out of it.

I push the paper back under the door before tapping slightly on the window, so they both look up at me. When they see me, I tap my wrist in the place where a watch would be if I was wearing one, a way of letting them know that they are to hurry up and not take too long answering this question. Then I step away from the window and give them some space to work.

Some space to save themselves.

Or condemn themselves.

24

DOMINIC

Kamilla and I stare at the question that has been asked of us by my wife, but neither one of us has had a real go at trying to answer it yet. We're both taking our time, and there's a good reason for that.

We can't afford to get it wrong.

Can you give me one good reason why I should let you go?

That's it. That's the question. It might seem simple enough, but it's a loaded one. The obvious answer is that Grace should let us go because it's the right thing to do. But something tells us she wants a bit more than that. She wants a real reason to let us go, one that doesn't just try and play to any sense of right and wrong that she might have left. But what can we give her?

'Tell her she'll go to prison if she doesn't open this door,' Kamilla says excitedly, as if she's just easily figured out the solution to a complex puzzle. 'That'll do it!'

'We don't want to antagonise her,' I remind my fellow prisoner.

'It's not antagonising her. It's reminding her that she will be facing serious time behind bars if she doesn't do it.'

'No, we need something else.'

'Like what?'

'I don't know!'

It feels like this whole situation has come down to us getting this right or wrong, like we're on some dodgy gameshow, and the host has just given us a 50/50 chance of winning the top prize.

Guess right and you will have your freedom.

But guess wrong and you'll never see the outside world again.

I've never been a fan of gameshows. There's too much luck involved, and invariably, the contestants lose. The game has to be rigged in some way. And it sure feels like this game is rigged right here.

'I don't think she wants to let us go,' I say sadly, after considering all the possibilities.

'What? She's just asked us to give a reason why she should.'

'I know, but that doesn't mean she wants to do it. It's like she's deliberately setting us up to fail. What are the chances we say the one thing she might want to hear? We could mention the police or how sorry and scared we are, or how she will never get away with what's she's doing, but she must have already considered all that, so it's not enough. She hasn't left us with much we can say.'

'So we don't just give one reason. Let's give them all,' Kamilla says defiantly, and she suddenly picks up the pencil and starts writing.

'What are you doing?'

'I'm covering all the bases.'

I watch as she writes several short sentences, but it's hard to read them with her hand still flying furiously across the paper, so I have to wait until she is done. It takes a while but eventually, she finishes, and when she does, I read her work.

Because you can't kill us.

You'll be a murderer if you leave us in here.

Our family and friends will be looking for us.

You'll get a life sentence.

You'll lose everything.

Everyone in this town will hate you.

You don't want to live with the regret of this.

You can't live with the regret of this.

If you don't open this door, you'll be looking over your shoulder for the rest of your life.

I have to give it to Kamilla. She's really gone for it with her answers. She's been less tactful and more like a bulldozer. Will it work? I'm not so sure.

'Push it under the door,' Kamilla urges me, already committed to what she's just done.

'Wait,' I tell her, re-reading the answers and wondering if some editing is needed. 'She only asked for one reason.'

'But there isn't just one! There are so many! And she knows it! You hear that? There's a million reasons why you have to open this door!'

Kamilla bangs on the door as she shouts at Grace, but that's not going to help matters, so I drag her away from it before she can make it worse.

'Just shut up and stay calm for one minute,' I beg her. 'We need to be smart here. This is not the time for acting on impulse.'

'No, it's the time for action. Serious action! Do you want to get out of here or not?'

'Of course I do.'

'Then put that note back under the door!'

'And what if she doesn't accept it? Where would that leave us? We have to make sure that what we say works. It might be the last chance we get.'

That last sentence hangs in the air, and I don't have to be a mind reader to know that after hearing it, Kamilla is thinking about all her loved ones and what it would mean if she was to never see them again. Not only that, but would they even know what had happened to her? Or would she just be listed as missing forever? Just like I might?

'Think, damn it. Think!' I say to myself as I pick up the pencil and grip it tightly. 'What do you want, Grace? What are you trying to get me to say?'

Thinking about the gameshows again, even though I know contestants rarely win, there is always the exception. Occasionally, somebody beats the odds. Somebody wins the game. Somebody gets the top prize and receives a hug from the host. I have to believe that I'm going to be that one winner.

So how do they do it? How do they win?

By taking a risk.

With that in mind, I start writing.

'What are you saying?' Kamilla asks me, but I ignore her as I write faster and faster, feeling a slight thrill at how bold I am being. If this was a gameshow, millions of people around the country would be tuned in to their TVs right now, wondering what I was going to do.

They'd just be about to get their answer.

'Okay, let's see if this works,' I say, and I fold the paper back up before going to the door.

'What is it? What did you say?' Kamilla pesters me but I ignore her but I make sure to deliver the note before I reply because I don't want to end up talking myself out of it. But once it's gone, and like a good gameshow host, I enlighten my audience so that they are fully up to speed with the progress of the game.

'I decided to stop being weak and go on the offensive,' I reply. 'As we're being bullied here and bullies only respond to shows of strength, I made sure to show Grace how strong we are. I told her that I lied earlier and that I don't regret the affair. I told her that I was bored with her, and I don't regret what I did because life is too short for regrets. And lastly, I told her that if I was to die in here with you over these next few days, then rather that than spending the next forty years having a miserable life with her.'

Kamilla's mouth hangs open after I've finished talking, and I get it. She's stunned. I've taken a massive gamble in what I've just said to my wife. But if we're going down, we might as well go down swinging.

'You're joking? Please tell me you're joking?'

Kamilla is getting very distressed, but I try to reassure her that it just might work.

'Begging and pleading won't get Grace to open this door,' I say, hoping I'm right. 'We've already tried that enough. But jealously might. Listen to this. There was a time once, back when we first started dating. We'd agreed to meet at the cinema at eight o'clock. But I'd got my times mixed up and ended up being half an hour late. Obviously, that's not a good thing to do in the early stages of a relationship, and I was worried I'd messed things up with Grace before they'd really got going. I thought she might be grumpy with me or maybe just go along with the date but not bother to arrange another one after it. But do you know what she did?'

'What?'

'After I'd arrived and apologised, I explained my honest mistake, and we went in to watch the movie. She didn't say much during the film, and it was only when we were walking out that I got a little insight into how her mind works. She said she had been worried that I'd been late because I'd got a better offer. Another woman to go on a date with or something like that. She told me she'd been imagining me meeting somebody else while she was standing there all by herself.'

'So?'

'So I realised then what she was most afraid of. It wasn't just losing somebody she liked. It was losing them *to somebody else*. She thought I had another woman that night, which I didn't. But now she knows for a fact that I do. But rather than try and apologise for getting caught, I should just own it. Yeah, I have another woman. What are you going to do about it, Grace?'

'She might keep us locked in here forever, that's what!'

'No, her jealously won't let her do that. It'll kill her admitting that she has lost me to you. But that's what will happen if she doesn't open this door. I'll forever be yours, not hers, if she does that, and she won't want it. I think this might work. I think she might let us out now.'

'What if she sees through it? What if she knows it's just a tactic?'

'She won't. I bet she's too blinded by jealously to see that.'

'Well, you better hope so because if it doesn't work, we have nothing!'

'It'll work,' I say with plenty of false bravado, but the nervous glance I make at the bottom of the doorway gives away my lack of confidence. There has been no reply from Grace yet. No reappearance of the note.

The gameshow audience has just gone very quiet.

The contestant might have just lost it all.

And then I hear it. A soft scratching on the ground. *The note is coming back.*

Both Kamilla and I pounce for it, but I'm the one who gets to it first, and as I eagerly unfold the paper, I know I'm at the moment where the gameshow host reveals the final outcome to the anxious contestant and nervous audience members. Has the dream become a reality? Will the door be unlocked? Will there be a winner after all?

Nice try. You know I'm the jealous type. But jealousy never did me any good, and it isn't going to get you out of this now. Goodbye, Dominic.

That's it.

The contestant knows it, and so does everybody watching.

It’s game over.

25

GRACE

TEN YEARS OLD

I was going to go and open the shed as soon as Mum had finished with the public appeal. I just needed a chance to sneak away so that I could do it without anybody knowing. But we didn't go home after the appeal. Instead, we went into a room with a detective, and they asked lots of questions about if Dad and Amy, the missing woman, knew each other.

But we weren't the only ones being asked. Amy's family was with us too, and I was sat next to Rosie and Joshua while Mum and Amy's husband started arguing. They were arguing because he didn't want to believe that an affair was going on, while Mum said it was obvious that it had been, and they had been left looking like fools.

The arguing got so bad that the detective had to end the meeting, and Mum and I watched as Amy's family were taken out of the room. I wondered if I would see Rosie again, but I didn't. What I did see, though, was Mum's face on TV when the appeal was shown several times on the news.

It was weird seeing my mum like that. Like she was a famous person. But she was famous. And then it got even weirder.

That's because I was on TV too.

There was a photo of me, Mum and Dad that kept getting shown on the news. I remembered when it was taken. It was at the zoo a year ago. I'm really happy in it because Mum had just let me have some candyfloss. That's why I'm holding her hand in the photo. I really loved her that day. I'm not holding Dad's hand in the photo though. That's because he had said no to the candyfloss because he thought it would spoil my dinner. He always used to say that whenever I wanted a treat. But Mum had been nice and let me have it.

Is that why I've been mean to Dad? Am I still annoyed at him for all the treats he didn't let me have growing up? Whatever my reason is for doing this, tonight is the night I am going to make it all stop.

It's been a week since I locked that door, but as soon as Mum goes to bed then I am going to sneak out of the house and go and open the shed. I'm a bit scared about going all that way in the dark, but I don't have a choice. I can't let anybody see me, and just like in a game of Hide and Seek, it'll be easier to stay hidden when there's no light.

I'm going to get out of the house by creeping downstairs, once I know Mum is asleep, and I'm going out the back door. I've been telling Mum not to put the alarm on at night when we go to bed in case Dad comes home, and she has finally given in and said she won't. That is how I can sneak out without her knowing.

I feel sick when I finally hear Mum come upstairs because I know the time has come for me to get ready to go. I'm already dressed, wearing clothes that will keep me warm when I'm outside. But just in case

Mum peeps into my room, I'm covered up by the duvet. But Mum doesn't look in on me. She just goes to her room, and after waiting a few minutes, I sneak to my door and look out to see if the light under her door is off.

It is.

I want to go immediately because I know I've already left it very late, but I wait a little longer to give her a chance to fall asleep. By the time I have crept to her bedroom door, I can hear her snoring on the other side of it. She's been snoring a lot lately. Maybe it has something to do with all those red drinks she keeps having. But it helps me tonight, and now all I have to do is stay quiet, and she'll never know that I've been gone.

It takes me ages to get down the stairs because I'm so worried about stepping on a creaky step and giving myself away, but once I've made it, it's easy to unlatch the door and get outside. It is cold out here, but I warm up as soon as I start running. It feels like I have such a long way to go but I have to do it or Dad will never get out of that shed and Rosie will never know what happened to her mum.

I think about her and wonder what she is doing now. I bet she's snuggled up in bed, safe and warm. I wish I was. It's spooky out here all by myself. A loud noise makes me jump, but I don't look back to see what made it. I just run faster, down one street and onto the next, only stopping and hiding whenever I see a car coming because I don't want the drivers to see me and stop to ask me why I'm out without my parents.

I thought I would feel a bit better when I got to the park, but I actually feel worse because it's even darker here than on the streets. There aren't any lights, and I can't see anything. I have to try and find my way by remembering where to go, but I keep getting it wrong and stumbling off the path and scratching myself on bushes and branches.

'Ouch!' I cry after bumping into a tree, and I rub my sore shoulder and try not to give up. 'Come on. You can do this.'

I keep going until I finally find my way to the shed. When I see it in the pale moonlight, it looks very dark and lonely.

And it's so quiet.

I had been wondering if I might hear Dad shouting for help, but there are no noises coming from inside the shed. Maybe they're both asleep. There wouldn't be anything else to do in there. But I'm sure they'll wake up when they hear the door open.

My plan is to unlock the door and then run away as quickly as I can, so they don't know who did it. I need to be fast, not just so I can escape without them seeing me but also so I can get back home before Dad does. I have to be in bed when he comes into the house, so I can pretend to be as surprised as Mum will be.

I creep up to the shed with the key in my hand and think about how all of this is going to be over soon. No more photos in the news. No more police asking questions. And no more seeing Rosie looking worried about her mum.

I put the key in the lock as quietly as I can, and then I stretch my arm out so that I'm as far from the door as I can be while still holding the key. I need to be out of here as soon as I turn it.

And then I do it.

With the door now unlocked, I abandon the key and run as fast as I can, sprinting down the path and around the bushes before the door opens and anybody calls after me. I run a little further but stop when I don't hear anything behind me.

Have they come out? I definitely opened the door. Maybe they just don't know it yet.

I stay where I am for a few minutes, waiting for the sound of footsteps behind me. But they don't come, so I creep back to the bushes and peep through them back at the shed.

The door is still closed.

Why aren't you coming out, Dad?

I keep waiting for the door to open because I can't go home until I know that Dad is definitely out of that shed. But he's not coming, and now I'm getting worried about him.

That's why I go back.

My heart is pounding as I put my hand on the door handle and slowly turn it, peering into the shed and trying to see inside even though it's so dark. I know I'm risking getting caught, but right now, I just want to see that Dad is okay. He might shout at me here if he does catch me but that's okay, I suppose. I just want him to be out now.

But he doesn't see me. That's because his eyes are closed. So are Amy's.

They are lying together on the floor, his arms around her.

They are asleep.

So I need to do something to wake them up.

I find a rock on the ground and throw it into the shed, and when it hits the wall opposite, I am certain they will wake up because it was so loud. But they still don't move.

Now it's time to shout.

'Dad! Wake up! I've found you!'

I want him to open his eyes. I want him to smile when he sees me. And I want him to hug me and thank me for saving him.

But he doesn't do any of that. He just keeps sleeping.

'Dad! Please, wake up!'

I'm in the shed now and shaking him, doing everything I can to get him to move. But he's so cold. So is Amy. What is wrong with them? Are they ill?

I think about how long they have gone without any food. They must be starving. And water? They haven't had any of that. Oh no, what if I have left them too long?

I keep shaking them and shouting, but nothing else happens. I'm still on my own out here, only now I am not scared of the dark.

I'm scared because I think I might have killed my dad.

26

GRACE

It's never got any easier. I can't forget what I did all those years ago, nor can I forgive myself.

I am responsible for the death of two people.

One of them was the man who helped raise me for the first ten years of my life. The other was a woman who had two children of her own to finish raising but never got the chance to.

How does a person live with something like that on their conscience?

The answer is with great difficulty.

I've barely managed it because every day has been a struggle. But I've held myself together enough to keep my terrible secret buried. No one knows how or why my dad and Amy came to be trapped inside that shed for so long that they died from dehydration. But here I am now, standing outside a cabin with two more people locked inside, and I am well aware that history is repeating itself. That's because despite wrestling with the decision of when to unlock this door and providing my prisoners with multiple chances to give me one good reason why I should let them out, I am still not any nearer to turning the key and giving them their freedom.

Maybe I should just put them out of their misery and walk away because it's clear to me now that I am going to do it again.

I am going to kill two more people.

Perhaps it's because I'm emboldened by the fact that I've got away with this once before that makes me think I can do it again. Maybe it won't be as bad this time. I'm an adult now, compared to a little girl when this happened before. I'm so much more mature now, not to mention composed. Not like when I was ten and ran all the way home crying after discovering that I was too late to save the couple in the shed.

I'm still not sure how I managed to make it back to my bed that night without Mum hearing me come in and catching me in the hallway with tears running down my cheeks and a guilty expression splashed all over my face. If only she had seen me then, if anybody at all had seen me, then I wouldn't have been able to stay quiet. I'd have confessed everything because I was an emotional wreck. But nobody saw me, so I was free to spend that whole night screaming into my pillow, and by the time morning came, I had shed every last tear that my body was capable of producing.

It took two more days of me living in a horrible world where I was the only person who knew what happened, before a dog walker passed by the shed, noticed the open door and went inside to make their grim discovery. After that, everything was a blur of stern police officers, awkward counsellors, weeping family and friends and a very sad-looking undertaker who went through all of Dad's funeral arrangements with Mum.

The day of the funeral was and still is the worst day of my life. Having to be so close to that coffin and knowing that I was responsible for its existence was hard, but what was even harder was seeing Mum glaring at it and not knowing how to react. Of course, she was upset that she had lost her husband, but she also knew that her husband's body had been found lying beside another woman, so her fears of an affair had been realised. That meant she hated Dad while she was also mourning him. It was no surprise, then, that all that conflict within her manifested itself in such a destructive way.

Mum had always liked a drink, but she really hit the bottle after Dad's death. It was as if she had been waiting for the universe to give her a good enough reason to drink herself into oblivion and boy, did she have it then. How could she not feel sorry for herself? She had become a widow and single mother overnight, and if that wasn't enough, she was bitter about what her man had been doing behind her back before his death.

I spent the rest of my school life having to fend for myself because Mum was useless after that. I sorted my own meals out, I got myself to and from school, and I had to be the one to pay the window cleaner whenever he came around for his money because Mum was usually way too drunk to answer the door to him or anybody else. If it hadn't been for the money that she got from Dad's life insurance pay-out then things might have been different because she would have been forced to get her act together and go back to work. But she made that money last a long time.

It didn't help her mood that the police spent a while suspecting Mum of having something to do with how Dad and his mistress came to be locked in that shed. They thought she might have instigated the pair getting trapped, as if it had been an act of revenge to punish them after she had discovered the affair earlier. But there was no evidence to back up their suspicions, just like there was none to back up their investigations into Amy's husband either. But while the police were busy looking at them, it meant they weren't looking at me.

Nobody suspected the little girl.

The sad daughter of the deceased.

The real criminal.

In the end, Dad and Amy's deaths were recorded as accidental. The police decided that they had gone to the shed to continue their affair but had inadvertently got themselves locked in and unable to escape, eventually succumbed to a lack of food and water over several torturous days. It was a grim explanation, but it was enough to stop the police looking at more sinister alternatives.

So, how does it feel to get away with murder? It's not as glamorous as it might seem. I certainly don't lay my head on my pillow every night with a smug sense of feeling like I have got one over on the people who set the law in this country. There was even a time in my early twenties when I felt like walking into a police station and confessing my crime, just so I could alleviate all my guilt and finally find some inner peace. But I didn't do that. Just as I was cowardly in not going back to that shed as a child until it was too late, I have been cowardly as an adult in going all these years without ever owning up to what I did.

Mum is still a heavy drinker these days, but I only know that because I have been to her flat a few times and seen the empty bottles on the windowsill on the other side of the glass, on show to anybody who passes by the property as if she is proud of how much she has consumed. Or maybe she just wants to make it obvious to anybody who might call around that it is not a happy home, so there's no point knocking on the door and expecting to receive a warm welcome.

It clearly works because nobody ever visits her. She's been successful in shutting everybody out over the years, most of all me, and while I'd love to have my mum in my life, I have learnt to accept that I just remind her of Dad, and she doesn't want any more reminders of him. I'm also sure that she partly blames me for his death, although not in the way of me being the one who actually locked the door. No, she will blame me because as far as she was concerned, Dad was happy with her before I came along. Having a child to raise made things more difficult for them. Less romantic. Less physical. He strayed; he accidentally got locked in a shed; he died. Mum must wish she had never had me because Dad might not have got bored with her if she hadn't, and she might still be with him today.

There is only one thing that is making me consider unlocking this door and letting Dominic and his woman out. It's the fear that I might end up just like Mum. Bitter. Angry. Alone. It's no way to be, but is it my future? Has it always been my fate? Was this always how my life was going to end?

I have to face it; I was never going to have a truly happy life after what I did when I was young.

With that in mind, is it even worth me trying to get away with this? Rather than trying to figure out a way to cover up what I am doing to my husband and his mistress, should I just put myself out of my misery and end my life? I won't end up like Mum then. And as for her, losing her daughter will certainly give her another excuse to pour herself another drink.

I'm just about to go back inside the house and figure out what my next move should be when I see the piece of paper come out from under the cabin door again. I hadn't been expecting a response from inside after the last note I left them, but as I pick the paper up, I see a new message has been written on it. But it's not in Dominic's handwriting. It's in hers. And what she has to say causes my hands to shake, my chest to tighten and my heart to skip a beat.

That's all before I let out the loudest and most bloodcurdling scream of my life.

27

DOMINIC

'What the hell did you write?'

My question to Kamilla comes after I heard my wife make the most guttural sound out in the garden just a moment ago. It was a noise that I've never heard her produce before. Come to think of it, I've never heard anybody produce a sound like that before, and I include characters in television and film in that too.

'I think I got her attention,' Kamilla replies as she looks out of the window. But Grace is no longer in the garden. She ran back into the house a moment ago and slammed the door behind her once she got there.

'I don't understand. What did you say?'

'I'll tell you soon.'

'Why can't you tell me now?'

'Because I don't know if it's worked yet.'

I have no idea why Kamilla is being so coy with me, but I have to give it to her. She has got a reaction out of my wife and while it might not have helped us get out yet, at least it has brought an abrupt end to this period of quiet hopelessness that we seemed to be stuck in.

'I've never seen her like that before,' I say. 'She didn't sound angry. She sounded hurt. Like seriously hurt.'

'I guess she knows how we feel now.'

We both hear another loud noise then, although this one is not as high-pitched and bloodcurdling as the last one. Rather, it's the sound of plates smashing in the house. The fact we can hear them from all the way down here means Grace is really putting some effort into hurling them at the walls. It also means that if we can hear it, the neighbours might too.

Frank and Maggie must have heard that scream. They had to, even if they had been asleep. We're pretty remote out here, and while we occasionally hear a fox or a bird after dark, nothing makes as much noise as Grace just made. With a bit of luck, they did hear it, and they have called the police to come and investigate. After all, people can't just ignore a scream at the best of times, but in the dead of night? That can never be good.

'It sounds like she's trashing the place,' Kamilla says from her position by the window.

More crashing and banging. A cry of pain. Or was it a roar? It's hard to tell. But Grace is still being very vocal, and that has to increase the odds of Frank and Maggie getting somebody to come and investigate.

While the thought of the police responding to a noise disturbance and arresting my wife is not ideal as far as my marriage goes, it's painfully obvious now that she needs some help. Psychiatric help. The best thing for her now is that she gets that help sooner rather than later, not just before she hurts us but before she hurts herself. At the moment, the only thing being hurt is all the crockery in the kitchen cupboards, but it can't be long until she moves onto something else, and it could be something that could cause her serious damage, if it hasn't been done already.

In stark contrast to my crazed wife in the house, my mistress is looking rather calm and collected.

'Tell me what you wrote. I have to know,' I urge Kamilla because the suspense is killing me.

'I just told her the truth,' comes the reply.

'And that is?'

'That she won't get away with this like she got away with it before.'

'What are you talking about?'

Kamilla looks at me, and I think she's going to elaborate, but she seems to stop herself before going any further.

'Hey, what do you mean like she got away with it before?'

Kamilla still doesn't answer me.

'Has she locked somebody else up? Is that what you mean?'

'Yeah, she locked you up, remember? In the hotel room with the handcuffs.'

She's right about that, but I can tell that isn't what she was referring to. There's something else. But what?

'What do you know about my wife? Did you know her before you met me?'

Another loud noise from the house. But Kamilla is quiet.

'Tell me! Did you know my wife? Is there something going on between you two that I don't know about?'

'Let's just say that tonight is not the first time I have seen her,' Kamilla says quietly.

'What's that supposed to mean?'

'It means I was aware of her before I met you, yes.'

'What is this all about?' I ask, struggling to keep up. 'Did you get with me to get back at her for something?'

'Kind of. But it's not as simple as that.'

'Then explain it to me!'

'I wanted to see if she had changed.'

'Changed?'

'I know what she used to be like. But I had to know if she was sorry and wouldn't do it again.'

'Sorry for what?'

'For what she did before.'

Both of us notice then that the noises in the house have stopped. What is Grace doing now? Is she still in there?

'What did she do before?' I ask, afraid of the answer.

'All I will say is that if you have been feeling like you're the bad guy in all of this, then it's time to stop that because your wife has you beat there, and she has you beat easily.'

Still no noise from the house. Still no indication of what Grace might be planning next.

'How is she the bad guy? I cheated on her.'

'Oh, come on, isn't it obvious now that she is seriously damaged?' Kamilla says. 'What kind of a person behaves like she has tonight? I'll tell you. A person who has done this before.'

'And how do you know she has done this before?'

'I just do.'

'You just do? What does that mean?'

Kamilla's calmness is more unsettling than my wife's eruption, and it's making me start to doubt everything I thought I knew about her.

'So you got with me to get to her? I was just a pawn in whatever crazy game you're trying to play?'

'I wouldn't put it as bluntly as that. We had some fun together, right?'

'Just tell me the truth? Have you been using me or not?'

It takes Kamilla a few seconds of saving my ego before she eventually nods and delivers it a damaging blow. So much for me thinking that I'd done well for a man of my age to attract the attentions of a woman her age. It turns out that just like Grace, I have been cheated too.

I try, but it's impossible to cover up how hurt I am to learn that I've been used, but when I think back over it all - how Kamilla and I met, how I made her laugh so easily, how she was seduced even though I've known I've always been a terrible flirt, it's so obvious now. I've been an idiot.

But if this has all been some kind of a game, how can Kamilla think she is winning?

'You're going to have to explain this to me because it's making no sense,' I say. 'If you're somehow trying to get back at my wife over something she's done before and you somehow set all of this up to hurt her, surely it has backfired? Because all you have managed to do is get yourself locked up, and Grace has the key, meaning she is winning, right?'

I can't see how I've stated anything but the obvious there, yet Kamilla just chuckles to herself as if this isn't a problem for her at all.

'What is one of the most important things to do before going into battle?' she asks me.

'I have no idea? What?'

'Know your enemy. And I sure know mine.'

'What's that supposed to mean?'

'It means I had anticipated something like this happening.'

'You thought you were going to get locked in here?'

'I thought there was a good chance if she caught us in the cabin, yes.'

'Why would you happily get yourself trapped like this?'

'Stop using the word trapped.'

'But that's the only word to describe this!'

'Trust me. Right now, Grace is the one who feels trapped.'

'How can you say that? She's out there while we're stuck in here!'

'But if given the choice of being me in here and her out there, I'd choose being me in here every time. That's because I have something she will never have.'

The loud noises begin again in the house, and it sounds like Grace is throwing much bigger things than plates this time.

‘What’s that?’ I ask as we both stand by the window, imagining the chaotic scene in the house before us.

‘I have a chance at happiness,’ Kamilla replies calmly. ‘But your wife most certainly does not.’

28

GRACE

It's taken some doing, but the inside of my home is now slowly starting to resemble the inside of my own head, and that means it is messy, chaotic and most of all, *broken.*

After throwing every plate and bowl that I could lay my hands on against the kitchen wall and watching them smash into a million pieces, I have now moved on to the more heavy-duty items, namely the chairs around the kitchen table. One after the other, I pick them up and swing them against the wall until the legs snap off and the back of the chair practically disintegrates in my hands. I used to love these chairs, and I paid good money for them when I bought them, but I couldn't care less about them now as they become just like everything else around here.

Seriously damaged.

Once the chairs are dealt with, I move onto the table itself. It will be no mean feat to break this thing, but I give it a good go anyway, using all of my strength to topple it so that it's no longer sitting sturdily on its four legs but lying awkwardly on its side, in a vulnerable position and ready for me to kick the legs off it until it will never be able to stand upright again.

I open the utensils drawer then, grabbing handfuls of cutlery before hurling forks, knives and spoons at the wall, screaming wild and incoherent noises as I do. I'm so angry that this reaction is the least I could do. But more than that, I'm in shock.

How could this happen?

How is it possible?

How could somebody know what I did all those years ago?

I still don't have any answers to those questions as I pick up the bread bin and throw it as hard as I can at the window. Amazingly, it doesn't smash the glass, but that doesn't mean the window is going to survive the night intact. There's still plenty of time for me to cause more damage here, and with the way I'm feeling now, I am certainly going to do that. That's because I'm scared about what all of this means. The words that Kamilla wrote on that paper aren't right in front of me at the moment, but I don't need to see them. They're already permanently etched on my brain.

I know this isn't the first time you locked two people up. KILLER.

That last word didn't need to be written in capitals for it to land with a big impact on me. It could have been written in tiny, almost unintelligible letters, and seeing it still would have shaken me to my core. How could it not disturb me? That woman in the cabin knows my darkest secret. She clearly knows what I did to Dad and Amy. But how?

The knock at the door has to be loud for me to hear it over all the things I'm throwing around in my kitchen, but it must be because I don't miss it, and the sound of it causes me to stop quickly.

Oh no. Somebody has heard me. It must be Frank or Maggie. I've been making far too much noise. They've come to check if everything is okay.

How can I even try and pretend to them that it is?

I want to leave their call unanswered, but the thought that they might just call the police makes me decide against it, so after closing the kitchen door so they won't be able to see all the damage in there, I open the front one and try to pretend like everything is fine.

But I don't do a very good job of it.

'Grace, what is going on? Is everything okay? We both heard all the noise, next door.'

Frank is standing on my doorstep, looking tired but concerned. A quick glance to my right helps me see the light on in his downstairs porch, and I can just about make out Maggie's silhouette standing in the hallway. She obviously sent her husband around here to make a quick check on things. Wow, I guess I really was being loud if they both heard me from over there.

'Grace? What is it? You can tell me.'

'I'm fine.'

'We heard a scream.'

'Did you?'

'Yes, was it you?'

'No.'

'Are you sure?'

'Yes.'

Frank looks over my shoulder into my house, but he won't be able to see anything to trouble him. But maybe he doesn't need to see anything behind me. Maybe the problem is written all over my face.

'Is Dominic home?' he asks me.

'What? No, he's working away, I told you.'

'Grace, you can tell me. Is something wrong?'

'Everything's fine.'

'Maggie said she was worried about you.'

'About me? Why?'

'She just wanted me to check on you.'

'Well, you've done that, so you can go now. Good night, Frank.'

I reach out to close the door, but when I do, I notice it. The drops of blood dripping from my hand onto my hallway floor. I must have cut myself in the kitchen when I was having my breakdown.

Frank has noticed it too.

'Are you hurt?'

'No.'

'You're bleeding.'

'I'm fine.'

'Do you want me to call Dominic?'

'No!'

'Is somebody else in the house with you?'

'What? No, of course not!'

'Can I just take a look?'

'Why would you want to do that?'

'So I can promise Maggie that everything is okay here. She won't stop worrying if not.'

There's no way I'm letting Frank in, but I need to give him something more than what I've just told him.

I need a story to explain the scream, and the noise, and the blood.

'I had a nightmare,' I say, shaking my head.

'A nightmare?'

'Yeah, it's silly, I know. How old am I? Too old to be having bad dreams, that's for sure. But that's what happened. I fell asleep on the sofa not long after Maggie left. Too much wine, I think. Anyway, I had a nightmare and woke up screaming. That would have been what you heard.'

'What about the blood?'

'I accidentally knocked the wine bottle off the table when I woke. It smashed, and I stupidly tried to pick up all the glass in my sleepy state. Managed to cut myself, didn't I? So silly of me.'

'Do you need to go to the hospital? I can drive you if you need me to.'

'No, I'll be fine. It's just a small cut. I think my pride is damaged more than my hand. I guess I just drank too much. My headache is worse than this cut, believe me.'

Frank looks a little sceptical, but I assure him again that I am fine until he takes my word for it and goes to leave.

'Okay, but if you need us, we're just next door.'

'Thank you, but I'm fine. I'll just get a plaster on this cut and then get myself off to bed, where I should have gone an hour ago.'

I smile weakly at Frank, and he returns the expression, but just like me, I can tell he's faking it. He doesn't say anything, though, just walking away back to his house, where I see the shape of Maggie move slightly at the window inside their home.

As I watch him go, I know it. I wish I didn't, but I do.

He doesn't believe me.

He knows I'm lying.

The question is: *what is he going to do about it?*

I close my front door but can't shake the anxiety around what Frank might be telling his wife when he gets back home. Most of all, I can't remove the fear that he might decide to call the police and have them make a quick check on me, just to be sure that I am really okay. Damn it, I should have been more convincing with my lie. The problem is, it was hard to do that with so much going on inside my head. But now I'm worrying about what is going on inside Frank's head. That's why I reopen my front door and step outside, hoping to see my concerned neighbour again. But he's already back at his house, and he's just about to go inside, where I presume he is going to tell his wife that he thinks something might be wrong with me.

Unless I can stop him from doing that.

Moving quickly, I pass through my front garden and into his, closing the distance between us and catching up with him before he can go inside.

'Frank! Wait a minute!'

He turns around when he hears my hushed call, and he looks a little startled to see me coming at him so quickly through the moonlight.

'What is it?'

The idea of attacking him so he can't go inside and potentially call the police is one that I entertain for the briefest of moments before I realise that it's too risky. Even if I could deal with him, there would still be the problem of Maggie. That's why I need to do something else.

I need to make this bored, middle-aged man feel like he can't tell his wife, or the police, that something might be wrong with me. How do I do that?

By making him need to keep a secret too.

'I just wanted to thank you for coming to check on me,' I tell him, smiling at him and doing a much better job of it than I did a moment ago. 'It's very kind of you to do that. You're a good man.'

I put a hand on his shoulder then, the hand that isn't leaking blood and a hand that he flinches at slightly. But he's not afraid. He's just not used to being touched by another woman.

'I-i-i-it's fine,' he stutters as he looks at my hand resting on his shoulder.

But I don't remove it. *I keep it there.*

'Maggie is so lucky to have a guy like you around to take care of her. You're not like my Dominic. I bet you don't leave your wife alone on the weekend to get all lonely, do you? I bet you take good care of her. I bet you could take good care of me too.'

My friendly smile has been replaced with a seductive one now, and Frank is growing more flustered by the second.

'I'll probably regret saying this in the morning, and maybe it's because I've had some wine tonight, but I have to tell you something. I've always had a bit of a crush on you, Frank. There, I've said it.'

It might be dark out, but I can see that he's blushing now.

'Oh my Gosh, please don't tell Maggie that I said that. Or Dominic. Can it be our little secret?'

I wink at him to try and seal the deal, and whatever Frank might be thinking now, I feel more assured of one thing. *He isn't thinking about calling the police anymore.*

'Oh, erm…I see. Erm…'

'I'm sorry, tell me if I'm out of line.'

'No, erm, not at all. Erm…'

Bless him, he's so awkward. I should let him go. But before I do…

'Thank you again for checking up on me. You're such a good man. I'm lucky to have you as my neighbour. And remember, if you could keep this as our secret, I would really appreciate that.'

'Of course.'

I wait for Frank to nod before I remove my hand from his shoulder, and now that I'm convinced he won't say anything to Maggie, or call the police, I walk away. With my neighbours dealt with, I return to my trashed home, and walking back into the kitchen again serves as a sobering reminder of the mental turmoil I was in just a few minutes ago. Being here, so close to the cabin and so close to the people locked inside it, is not good for me.

I need to get out of here.

I need to leave.

I grab my car keys and head back to the door but I'm not leaving until I have made sure that all the lights are off at Frank and Maggie's. They are. They must have gone to bed. Frank has kept his word to me.

Our little secret.

Confident that the police won't be calling around here tonight after all, I get behind the wheel and start the engine before reversing off my driveway and heading onto the dark, country lanes. I don't have a particular destination in mind; I just need space and time to think.

I already know that I can't unlock the cabin door now. That can't happen. They both have to die in there. But what about me? Should I just leave? I could get pretty far before Frank and Maggie stick their noses into my business again and realise that their neighbours seem to be missing. Maybe I'll just drive down to Dover and get on a ferry to France. But I'd need my passport for that, and I left it at home. Damn it. What about Scotland? I could go up there, lie low, use a false name, maybe even start again.

As I'm running through all my options, I fail to notice that I'm no longer alone on the road. There's a car behind me, and despite how fast I am driving, and how erratically I am taking these tight, twisting bends on these country lanes, they are keeping up with me.

But I don't notice them doing that.

I only notice them when the blue flashing lights come on.

29

GRACE

‘Have you had anything to drink tonight?’

The question from the police officer standing in front of me is an easy one to ask but not an easy one to answer. That’s because I can’t tell the truth. I have consumed alcohol this evening, and he probably knows it, although not for sure until he makes me do a breathalyser test. But there’s a reason why he made me stop by this roadside, and it wasn’t to compliment me on my driving skills.

It was to try and find out why they were so bad.

‘A drink? Me? Erm…’

‘Just wait here, please.’

I watch as the police officer returns to his vehicle, the one that I had really wished I’d noticed behind me earlier so I could have slowed down and made it less obvious that I was driving under the influence. But it wasn’t the wine that caused me to speed. It’s what was written on that note.

It’s what that woman in the cabin knows about me.

But that doesn’t matter now. All that matters is that this police officer is going to make me blow into a tube in a moment’s time, and when I do, he’ll see that I am over the drink-drive limit thanks to all that wine I had with Maggie earlier, and then he will put me in handcuffs and drive me to the police station.

So I should run. Get back behind my wheel and drive away. He'll chase me, of course, but he might not catch me.

But the fact that I'm still standing uselessly by the side of my car when he returns means I didn't do that, and now it's too late because he has the breathalyser, and he's giving me the instructions for how to use it.

'Is this really necessary?' I ask him. 'I'm sorry if I was going a little too fast. I'm just trying to get home. I'm sorry, it won't happen again.'

But he just holds out the breathalyser, and I stare at the white tube in front of me, knowing what I have to do but afraid to do it.

That's why I start crying.

'I've had the worst day,' I moan, not actually having to lie, which makes it even easier to get upset. 'Work has been hell, I'm exhausted, and on top of all of that, I'm waiting for some test results from my doctor. He's really worried about me. I think something is seriously wrong.'

Maybe this will work. Maybe the policeman will take pity on me and let me go home with just a warning. It's got to be worth a shot.

'Please, can I just go home? I'm sorry. I'll never speed again. Please, I just want to go home.'

Home is the last place I want to be, but it's preferable to a prison cell, so I'll take my chances, and amazingly, the policeman seems to be considering my plea. Or at least he does right up until the moment he repeats his instruction for me to blow into the tube.

Five minutes later and I'm sitting in the back of his police vehicle after failing the test and proving that I have been drink-driving tonight. I'm so stupid. I never should have driven. But what were the chances of encountering a police officer on these lanes, at this time of night? How unlucky can I be? But it only takes me a second to remember everything I've been through to get my answer to that.

I don't say a word as I'm driven to the police station, and when I get there, I only speak to confirm my name, date of birth and address. That and informing the arresting officer that my husband is working away this weekend, so I'd prefer it if he didn't find out about this. Thankfully, they aren't going to call my house or pay a visit there, so there's no danger of them discovering my sordid secret in the cabin just yet. But there's not much more to be happy about as I'm led into a cell where I am told I will spend the night while I sober up.

As I watch the key turn in the lock, I finally get a sense of how my husband and his mistress must have felt when they realised I was locking them in the cabin. I also know how my dad and Amy would have felt all those years ago too.

Trapped.

Helpless.

Scared.

How could I have done this to other people? And more importantly, why? There's nothing quite like a long, lonely night in a police cell to make one think about their life choices and regret what has gone before, and that's how I spend my evening. But there's one incident in particular that I keep thinking back on. It's a time when perhaps I should have realised that I hadn't changed and done something about it while I still had the chance. If only I had acted, there is a good chance none of this would be happening now.

But I didn't. I ignored the warning sign. Most amazingly of all, my husband ignored it too. If only he had left me after it happened, he could have spared us both of this. He wouldn't have been with me long enough after it to cheat on me. He wouldn't have ever met that woman and caused me to lock them away. And I would never have had to know that somebody else knew my secret.

But now I know.

That night when I handcuffed Dominic to the bed in the hotel room in Bath and went out for dinner without him was my chance. It was my chance to realise that I was forever fated to react badly to anyone who might have done me wrong and realise that the only way I could avoid causing pain and misery in the future was to avoid other people altogether. Instead, I just breezed straight past the warning sign and sat in that restaurant, ordering food, drinking wine and feeling like I was the one in the right.

How very wrong I was.

30

GRACE

FOUR YEARS AGO

'I can't quite choose between the salmon and the trout,' I say to the attentive waiter standing beside my table, in the hope that he will give me his recommendation. And sure enough, he does.

'May I suggest the salmon? It is our most popular dish.'

'The salmon it is. Thank you.'

I hand the menu back to him and smile as he walks away, but I know it won't be long until he is back. He's been to my table every five minutes ever since I sat down in this restaurant to make sure that I am having the best meal I can. Or maybe it's because he can see that I'm dining alone and wants to make sure that I'm not feeling too lonely throughout the duration of my meal. But whatever reason for him to keep giving me such good service, I'll take it.

I've never sat in a restaurant by myself before. I guess the thought never occurred to me to go and eat out if I had no one to eat with. Plus I was probably a little self-conscious about contemplating doing such a thing because it's not an easy thing to do to sit alone surrounded by other people who are seated together.

I'm sure some of the diners here have been wondering why I'm not with anyone. Perhaps they think

I've been stood up by my potential date. Or maybe they think I can't even get a date and have no choice but to go out alone on a Saturday night in Bath.

If only they knew the real reason.

If only they knew that I could be with somebody right now, but I've chosen to handcuff them to the bed in the hotel room and refused to let them out for dinner tonight.

I think about my captive husband as I swill the red wine in my glass and eagerly await the arrival of my salmon. Dominic must be so hungry now. There'll certainly be no tasty meal for him this evening. I bet he regrets neglecting me all day. This will teach him. He won't make the same mistake again.

Sure enough, it doesn't take long for the waiter to come back to see me and when he does, he asks if I am enjoying the wine.

'It's lovely, thank you.'

'Could I interest you in a second glass?'

'Possibly. I'll see what kind of mood I'm in after my starter.'

'No problem.'

The waiter leaves again, and now he's at one of the tables nearby, talking to the couple seated there. I feel slightly envious because I should have been enjoying a romantic meal this evening before my partner screwed it up. Was it too much to ask for him to forget about work on a Saturday and give me 100% of his focus? Evidently so, or he'd be sitting opposite me now holding his own glass of wine. But despite knowing that he should have treated me better today, there is something gnawing away at the back of my mind. It's the awareness that despite what happened so many years ago with my father and despite telling myself that I would never do anything like it again, my first reaction to being hurt was to trap Dominic.

I've spent many years trying to convince myself that what I did to Dad and Amy was just the actions of a confused, scared kid. After all, is there ever really a right way for a ten-year-old to react to catching their father with another woman? There were a million ways I could have responded, and I just did what came to me in that moment. But I'm an adult now, so what's my excuse this time? That's why despite all the years of telling myself it was a one-off, I think the reality is painfully clear now. I am somebody who gets a thrill out of trapping people in situations where I'm the only one who can free them. But it's not a sexual thrill or even a fun one. It's just what I do.

Anybody can do something once.

But twice is a pattern.

Anymore and it will become a habit.

Will I have to do this again? Not if Dominic doesn't do anything to hurt me, which remains to be seen. But I clearly have a demon inside me, a part of me that tells me to do these things. Should I seek help for that before I go too far again and kill somebody? No, I can't, the risks would be too high. If I admit to a medical professional about what I like to do, they might figure out that it was most likely me who trapped my dad all those years ago. I can't risk that. I suppose I could give a false name so she couldn't make the link to my deceased parent, but if I'm having to do that, it's already a sign that I shouldn't be talking to anybody about it.

I guess I'll just have to figure this out on my own.

But what I've done tonight is not the same as what I did when I was ten. I am going to free my prisoner, and I'll do it soon, right after I finish my meal. There's no threat to life this time. So maybe that earlier incident was a one-off. This is hardly in the same league. In fact, the more I think about it, the more I realise that it's not even that different to what I'm sure has happened in plenty of other relationships besides mine. Plenty of people use handcuffs to restrain their partners in the bedroom. Some people even pay good money to have it done to them. I bet there's some in this restaurant who are no stranger to being restrained in a hotel room. Am I really that different to them?

Not if I don't take it any further.

The sight of my salmon being carried towards me on a well-presented plate by the smiling waiter takes my mind off Dominic and the fact that I have prevented him from being with me to have his food. By the time the fish is placed down in front of me and I have asked for that second glass of wine after all, I am feeling confident about the future.

This won't happen again because Dominic won't hurt me. He'd be a fool to do so after finding out what I'm capable of.

This is just a warning to him. Nothing more and nothing less. And it's one that I am sure he will heed.

But would him heeding it be better for his sake?

Or for mine?

31

GRACE

With all that I have done in my past, the last thing I needed was a long, lonely night trapped in a cell to give me time to think about things. But that's what I got, meaning the issue of being caught driving while over the limit is actually the least of my worries.

I've not spent these last few hours afraid of other people and what they might do to me. I've been more worried about myself and what I might do if I have to endure many more nights like this last one. While I am only being detained in the short term while the alcohol leaves my bloodstream and while I'll most likely lose my driving licence for being out on the roads while under the influence of something I shouldn't have been, the real issue is making sure the police don't discover the couple in the cabin.

If being in here has taught me anything, it's that I am not cut out for prison. I guess I always knew that, or I wouldn't have been so afraid about coming clean over what I did to Dad. But it's been confirmed now, and that's why all I want to do is get home, away from all these officers, where I can check on my prisoners and maybe, just maybe, let them go.

They're not worth it. Certainly not worth me spending the rest of my life behind bars for. So what if I unlock that door and they come straight down here to tell everybody in this police station what I did to them? I'll just deny it. All I'll have to do is quickly tidy the cabin up once I've let them out, and there won't be much in the way of evidence that anyone was ever held against their will there. I'm sure I'll get away with it, or at least I'm surer of getting away with it than if I leave them in there to die.

I have no idea what time it actually is when I see a police officer appear on the other side of the bars and put a key into the lock.

'What's happening?' I ask him, even though it's obvious at that point that he is letting me out.

'You're going home,' he replies with all the weariness of someone who is coming to the end of their night shift. 'We can call for somebody to pick you up or an officer will take you back to your house. Your car has been detained on account of you not being fit to drive anymore. And you've still been charged with drink-driving, so this isn't over yet.'

I want to agree with the policeman about this not being over yet, but I don't because I wouldn't be referring to the crime he is talking about. So I just say nothing as I stride out of the cell and tell myself that I'm on my way to being back home now, so I shouldn't grumble about being released.

After the personal items that were on me at the time of my arrest have been handed back to me, I'm asked if there is anybody to be called to come and collect me.

'No, nobody,' I say, and the policewoman behind the counter probably assumes that I'm too ashamed to call a friend or family member to come and get me, so I'm happy to let her keep thinking that. I'm then told that a police officer can take me home, but I refuse that option and say I'll be fine getting a taxi.

The sense of judgement coming from the woman opposite me is strong. I'm sure she is thinking that if I didn't want to be seen by my neighbours being taken home in a police car then I shouldn't have broken the law, but whatever. She doesn't need to know that I just have to do anything I can to keep the police away from my house until I've unlocked that cabin door.

It's a relief to leave the police station, and while I wait for my taxi, I'm taken back to when I was a teenager and how frustrating it felt to not be able to drive. It feels like I've lost one of my biggest freedoms, and I guess I have.

My husband and my driving licence in just a couple of days.

What else is going to be taken from me before this is all over?

The driver of the taxi I get into is surprisingly quiet as he takes me home, but I guess it's because he can hardly ask me how my day is going if he's just picked me up from outside a police station. The few glances he makes in his rear-view mirror at me on the back seat probably tell him that I haven't slept much, so he might be able to guess that I've had a bad night. No need for small talk here then. Just keep driving.

I'm praying that I won't see Frank or Maggie when we get back because they'll surely have some questions about why I'm in a taxi and not my car. If I do see them, I'll just have to say something about my car breaking down in town and how it's at the mechanic's now. But they aren't there when I arrive, so I am free to go inside without further delay.

I grab a bottle of water from the fridge to soothe my parched throat while I survey the messy scene around me. This kitchen is destroyed. I really went for it last night. But there will be time for cleaning up later. Right now, this is not it.

I waste no more time and before I chicken out, I decide that am going to that cabin and opening the door.

I pick up the key and head out into the back garden, warmed slightly by the weak sunshine that is currently bathing my back garden in its yellow hue. But then my entire body turns cold when I see what is waiting for me at the bottom of the garden.

'No,' I cry as I start sprinting towards the cabin, but even before I get there, I already know it's too late.

That's because the cabin door is wide open.

Somehow it has been unlocked, and because it has, I'm sure the two people inside have already gone.

How has this happened? It's impossible.

They were trapped.

But now they are free.

I reach the open door and stop running, needing a second to pluck up the courage before I go inside and confirm my worst fears. If they have gone, there is no telling where they might be now. At the police station? Already sitting opposite a detective who is getting their statements on tape? Or in a police car that is racing here with an officer who is coming to arrest me? The paranoia that comes from the uncertainty of it all is overwhelming as I step into the cabin and have my worst fears confirmed.

The cabin is empty.

Dominic and the woman are gone.

This situation is no longer controlled.

I'm just about to make a run for it and get as far away from here as possible to try and evade whatever police officers are going to be chasing me soon when I hear it.

The sound of the door closing behind me.

I race towards it, but it's too late. The next sound is of a key turning in the lock, and even though I try the handle, the door doesn't budge.

I'm now the one trapped in the cabin.

I'm now the one getting a taste of my own medicine.

But who is my captor?

All it takes is me going to the window to find out.

32

GRACE

All this time trying to keep people inside this cabin, and now I'm the one trapped in it. There are three people staring back at me from the other side of the glass. One of them I know very well; one of them I have met once and who did me a favour on that occasion, and the other who I have spent the last few days hating and only interacting with via a series of scribbled notes.

Three people who are together while I'm in here.

Three people who seem to be working as a team against me.

Three people who have the upper hand.

But how?

'Dominic! Open this door!' I cry, trying my husband first because he might be the only one whom I can trust. But he says nothing, nor does he make any move towards the door, letting me know that I'm going to have to try my luck with the other two if I'm hoping to get somewhere.

The person standing beside him is the woman I locked him in here with, but the sadistic smile on her face offers no sense of quick resolution either. I still don't know her name, nor do I know how she found out what I did in the past, but the more she smirks at me, the more I get the feeling that she had the upper hand all along. But it's the man standing on the other side of her that really confirms that fear.

It's Clark, the man I met at my work event on the night I found out Dominic was having an affair and the man who gave me a ride home just before I walked into this cabin and caught my husband at it with this woman.

But what the hell is he doing here?

He doesn't look sad like my husband or smirky like his mistress. He just reaches into his pocket and takes out a mobile phone, and after he puts it to his ear, I hear my own phone start ringing in my coat pocket.

I realise Clark is calling me, so I answer quickly.

'Clark? What are you doing here?' is my first question, but I have plenty more where that came from. I need to unravel the mystery of why the man who met me at a networking event is now standing in my back garden, looking like he always knew he was going to end up here.

'Who's Clark?' comes the chilling reply as we stare into each other's eyes with our phones by our right ears.

'What? That's your name! We met at the event!'

'I'll admit I wasn't exactly honest with you,' Clark, or whatever his name is, replies. 'Just like you haven't been honest to so many others.'

'What are you talking about?'

'I'm talking about your father,' he says, and I go so weak then that I almost drop the phone at my feet.

Why has he just mentioned my father? But then I think of what Dominic's mistress wrote in her note to me. How she called me a killer. Now it's clear that she isn't the only one who knows what I've done.

This man know too.

'My father? What are you talking about?' I try, hoping to maintain my secret despite the futility of it.

'I'm talking about how you locked him away. I'm talking about how you let him die. Him and the woman he was with.'

It's confirmation that the worst thing I have ever done is now exposed. My awful secret is out in the open. Now it is, I look to Dominic to see how he is reacting to all of this. But he doesn't look shocked or surprised. He still just looks very sad, as if he has accepted what he has heard about me, just like he is now accepting whatever punishment these two people seem to have decided on for me.

But what might that be?

'That's right, Grace. We know what you did when you were ten. You locked your father in that shed. You locked him in there because he was with another woman. And you've done the same thing again here. History has a funny habit of repeating itself, doesn't it?'

There's no point in me denying it now because he clearly knows the truth. What I need to do is find a way out of here before he can share his knowledge with the police, whom I'm guessing he hasn't spoken to yet or else I would already be in custody. *Proper custody, not this improvised kind.*

'Who are you?' I ask, racking my brains for an answer but not able to figure out who might have been capable of unearthing this secret from so many years ago.

'I'm another one of your victims,' comes the calm reply through the phone. 'I'm another person your actions hurt. More specifically, I'm the son of the woman you killed when you chose to lock the door to that shed over thirty years ago.'

It takes me a couple of seconds before the awful truth dawns on me.

He's Amy's son.

Clark is Joshua.

'No,' I utter, the word escaping my mouth along with what feels like all the air in my lungs.

'Yes,' Joshua replies. 'You killed my mother. It's taken us a long time to figure it out, but it was you. You were the only other person who knew about that shed. Do you know how I found that out? I went to see your mum. It was three months ago. I tracked her down online and went to talk to her. I wanted to see how she was doing. Wanted to see if she was still struggling to cope with what happened all those years ago. And guess what, she was. In fact, she seemed to be suffering more than me.'

I don't need Joshua to tell me how bad my mother has had it since my father died, but I do need to know what they talked about.

'What did you say to her?' I ask, wondering if it might have been Mum who put the idea in his head that I had something to do with Dad's death, even though I've always felt that she had no idea, just like the police didn't either.

'It wasn't what I said to her but what she said to me. It took me a little while to get in her house. She turned me away at first when I told her who I was. Said she didn't want to be reminded of that cheating man and his mistress and told me to get lost. But I could clearly see that she was drunk, so all I had to do was go to the nearest supermarket, pick up a few bottles of booze and surprise surprise, the next time I knocked on her door, she was more receptible to a guest.'

My hand grips the phone as I stand shaking in the cabin, desperate to get out and get away from this man who knows too much.

'I genuinely wanted to just talk to her,' Joshua goes on. 'I had no agenda. I just wanted to go over what happened when I was a kid. As you know, I was only thirteen when my mum died. Too young to really understand everything. I tried talking to my dad about it as I got older, but he just shut me down straight away. Do you want to know what happened to him, by the way? He met someone else, moved on quickly just to get over the pain. But he never did because he never really got over Mum. He was bitter, and he stayed that way until he died from a heart attack two years ago. So now I have no parents, and neither does my sister, Rosie.'

The mention of the little girl, a person who I once thought might be my friend, has me thinking back to the day I met her and her brother at the press conference. Things were so different then. We were all so young. And Dad and Amy were probably still alive in that shed.

'Where is Rosie?' I ask, not that it matters, but I have to know.

'She couldn't be here today,' Joshua tells me calmly. 'Actually, I'm not being honest. She could be here today, but she chose not to be. She said she couldn't trust herself around you after what you did. But while she isn't here, someone very close to her is. Meet Kamilla, Rosie's daughter.'

'I finally have a name to put to the face of the woman who has been sleeping with my husband, but it's not the name I give a damn about now. It's who she is. *Rosie's daughter.* That little girl I met whilst surrounded by so many police officers and journalists at the appeal has grown up and had a child of her own, and now that child is standing right in front of me as a young woman herself, a young woman who has slept with my husband. But I'm guessing it wasn't just any old affair now. I'm guessing she seduced Dominic to get closer to me. And sure enough, Joshua confirms that.

'Your husband isn't quite the stud he thought he might have been,' Joshua says, glancing at Dominic and offering an apologetic shrug. 'But don't worry, we've explained everything to him, and he's on our side now.'

'What do you mean you've explained everything to him?'

'Your dad. Our mum. You trapping them. Come on, Grace. Keep up, or else you'll never get out of there.'

'How do you know?' I ask, still unsure and still so very scared of what might happen now my secret is out.

'As I mentioned, I went to see your mum, and we were talking about our loss. It was mainly me doing the talking on account of how drunk your mother was as she sat opposite me and swigged from a bottle. But it was during our conversation that she said something very interesting. I had asked her, out of genuine curiosity, if she really had no idea about that shed her husband had. After all, she had told the police at the time that she didn't, but she might have been lying, right? Well, she again confirmed that she wasn't aware of its existence, and I believed her, even through the alcohol, so I felt confident she wasn't the one who had locked that door. And then I asked her about you.'

'Me?'

'Yes. I asked her if you might have known about the shed.'

Mum must have said no. She didn't know that I knew. It was mine and Dad's secret. Well, mine, Dad's and Amy's, at least.

'She said that you didn't know about it either,' Joshua tells me, which sounds promising. 'But then she said something else when I asked her what your relationship with your father was like. She said that you were closer to him than her before he passed away. More of a daddy's girl as you got older. She mentioned how the pair of you would sometimes go out together on Sunday afternoons. Daddy and daughter time. He would try and cheer you up because you used to get bullied. But when I pressed her on it, your mum could not say where you went. Because she didn't know. But that's when I got to thinking, I wonder if you went to that shed. I wonder if your dad had let you in on his secret hiding place.'

‘This is all speculation,’ I say because even though it’s not, I could argue it is in a court of law.

‘Yep, I’m sure that’s what you would say to the police if I went to them with these accusations,’ Joshua tells me with a nod of the head. ‘What I would need for this theory of mine is evidence.’

‘Which you don’t have.’

‘Oh, are you sure about that?’

I don’t like Joshua’s confidence.

‘Your mum ended up falling asleep as we were talking,’ he goes on. ‘Some people might get offended by that, but I didn’t mind. It gave me the chance to have a look around her home. It was extremely untidy, as I’m sure you knew. Years of neglect. But despite the general state of the place, your mother had made sure to keep certain memories in an organised fashion. Memories from a time before her family had fallen apart. I found several photo albums with some old pictures in. Most of them were fairly boring. Family things. Baby pictures. The three of you at the seaside. Your dad building your crib. All very normal and average. Until I found this one.’

Joshua produces a photo then and slams it against the window, allowing me to see the image through the glass, and when I do, I see my younger self standing beside a small body of water.

‘Recognise this?’ Joshua asks me. ‘I’m not talking about the girl in the picture because we know that’s you. I’m talking about the water behind you. Where is it?’

I know exactly where it is, but I'm not going to say. Unfortunately, Joshua has the answer anyway.

'I'll tell you where it is. It's the lake in Rydal woods. It's the same lake that the shed was sitting beside. The shed that held the bodies of our parents.'

I still say nothing, but my silence is surely proof that I am not disagreeing.

'I recognised the lake as soon as I saw it, but I had to be sure,' Joshua goes on. 'So I took this photo from the album and left your mum sleeping on her sofa, and I went straight down to the woods. I went to the shed, that place I used to hate so much. Have you any idea how horrible it was for me to go there? The place where my mum died? It was awful. But I had to do it. I had to see if the landscape in the background of this photo matched the landscape behind the shed. And guess what? It did.'

I notice that I look so young in the photo. Happy too. I guess that's because I was innocent then.

'This is proof that you had been to that shed before,' Joshua claims. 'Your dad took this photo of you there. Your mum has never noticed it amongst all the others, but I did, and with it, I knew you were lying. You told the police you didn't know about that shed. But you did, so there had to be a good reason why you lied. The reason was because you locked that door, didn't you? You killed them. It was you.'

I'm still not saying anything, but Joshua can see me easily enough through the window and because he can, he hasn't failed to notice the tears running down my cheeks. But he's not done with me yet.

'As soon as I suspected you, I went to my sister. I said we had to tell the police. But do you know what she said. She said I might be wrong. Maybe you hadn't done it. She wanted to give you a chance. A chance to prove you might not be capable of such a thing. So she came up with an idea. She wanted to put you to the test. She wanted to see how you would react if you were ever to stumble across the same thing again. Two people who shouldn't be together, one of whom you cared deeply about. Would you react like a normal person and just shout and scream? Or would you do something else, something like locking the door and keeping them prisoner? Well, we all know which option you chose now, don't we?'

'You set this whole thing up to test me?' I ask, finding my voice again through the tears.

'Yes, we did,' Joshua confirms. 'Rosie and I made the plan. We had Kamilla seduce your husband, and once the affair had developed, we knew she could eventually persuade Dominic to carry out their illicit activity somewhere with a lockable door. Like this cabin at the bottom of your garden, for instance. All we had to do then was make sure you came home and caught them together. That's where I came in. I wasn't at that networking event by chance that night. I was there to befriend you and more importantly, I was there to make sure you went home rather than stayed in a hotel. We needed you to catch them together. And we needed to see how you would react. All you had to do was not lock this door. If you hadn't, I might have considered that my theory was wrong, and maybe you hadn't killed our parents. But you proved my theory right. You proved that you were capable of acting irrationally and dangerously. The course of action you chose is now the reason you're stuck in there. And it's the reason you'll be spending a lot of time under lock and key going forward, once the police get here to arrest you.'

Joshua finally stops talking then and lowers his phone, clearly happy to show me that he has said all he needs to, and he feels like there is nothing more to be discussed. But I have something to say, so I point to my phone so he knows to put his back to his ear. And then I give it to him, not an apology or a congratulations on catching me. Instead, I give him the words of a woman still confident she can get out of this without punishment.

'Fine. I admit it. I did it. I locked that shed, and I'm the one to blame for the deaths. I know it, and I've lived with it all this time, which is punishment enough, let me tell you. But I'm not going to go to prison because I'm not admitting this to the police. You can't prove it. All you have is that photo, and if that's your best bet, good luck because I'm sure I can find a lawyer who can argue it doesn't prove I did it. All it proves is that I was at the lake once. But not the shed. So go for it, give it to the police and tell them how crazy I am. But I'll be fine. I've got away with murder for thirty years, and I have a feeling I'll keep getting away with it for a lot longer than that.'

It's now my turn to lower my phone, but I go the extra mile now and actually end the call before tossing my device onto the desk behind me and shrugging my shoulders, displaying to everybody outside that I am done. I'm not worried about the police, nor am I worried that they might decide to keep me locked up in here forever because Dominic won't let them, and even if he did, they'd never all get away with it. I got lucky once, but they won't.

So they have to open this door. They have no choice.

It takes a little while, but Joshua seems to realise that because after having a discussion with Kamilla, he looks at the door and shakes his head. Then he makes his way over, and I get ready to enjoy my freedom once again. This will be the second time this morning that I've been let free to go, and just like the first time, I'm going to enjoy it.

The key turns in the lock before the handle moves, and more daylight suddenly seeps in. With the door open, I step towards it, but before I can get there, Joshua walks in.

I suddenly worry that he might be about to attack me, a violent outburst being his only way of getting revenge on me now. But he doesn't do that. All he does is walk over to the shelf above the desk and move one of the books up there. When he does, I see a small device with a blinking red light.

'Is there anything else you'd like to say before I turn this recording device off?' Joshua tells me as he holds it up for me to get a better look. 'Or is admitting to getting away with murder for thirty years quite enough for one day?'

33

DOMINIC

THREE MONTHS LATER

The cabin had to go. That was obvious, and as I stood in my back garden and watched a team of labourers dismantling it, I couldn't help but wish I'd never had it built in the first place. No cabin would have meant no chance for all of the horrible things to have happened. I couldn't have been locked in there. Neither could Grace. And ultimately, I probably would have never found out that my wife was a murderer.

As the once impressive structure is broken down into smaller, more manageable pieces of timber and each one is carried from the garden to the back of a truck parked on the driveway, I feel an enormous sense of loss. But it has nothing to do with thinking about all the future times I have lost in that cabin. I'm not bothered about no longer having a quiet place to work from home or an isolated place to watch some television and have a beer. The end of my 'man cave' is not what is giving me grief. Rather, the loss I feel is over my marriage and the fact that the woman I married is no longer here, nor is she likely to ever be again.

It's been a wild time, and I sometimes think it started with me embarking on my affair with Kamilla. But in truth, it really got wild when I discovered she was not just some colleague who had taken a shine to me but rather a very clever and manipulative woman who had sought me out on purpose with only one real intention.

To get closer to Grace.

As soon as I started to realise that in the cabin while trapped with Kamilla, the more time seemed to speed up. After going so slowly for the initial period while I was kept prisoner, the minutes and seconds seemed to triple in speed once Kamilla told me how she had written a note to my wife in which she called her a killer, before explaining exactly why she had given her that moniker.

The story of what Grace had allegedly done to Kamilla's grandmother, and her own father at the same time, was shocking. How could the tale of a little girl locking two people in a shed and leaving them to die be anything but? But it was also strangely familiar because once I thought about it, I could see that it was definitely something my wife was capable of. She'd locked me up, twice, in fact, so why couldn't she have done it to someone else? That's why I'd told Kamilla that I believed her when she told me what Grace had done all those years ago. But even then, I hadn't seen how it helped us in our current plight.

But that was where Kamilla had surprised me again because she told me that she had only been acting desperate ever since getting locked in the cabin. In reality, she had always known she could get out of here at any time, and the reason for that confidence was because she had somebody helping her on the outside. That somebody was her uncle Joshua, and he made an appearance shortly after, striding into my back garden, lifting up the plant pot and removing the spare cabin key from beneath it before putting it in the lock and opening the door with the minimum of fuss. As the door was opened, Kamilla told me that they had been watching this house for some time, which was how they knew not only about the cabin but where I kept the spare key.

I also discovered once I was released that the man who had opened the door had been keeping watch over my house and cabin ever since we had been locked up. He'd been tracking Grace's movements and when I asked him where my wife was, he told me she was in police custody. He explained that he knew she had been drinking so when she left the house and drove off, he made a quick call to the police, passing on the car's registration plate and his concerns that the driver was inebriated, well aware that Grace would be stopped, breathalysed and arrested. Taking her off the streets for a temporary time gave him the chance to come and unlock the cabin and get the next part of his plan in motion, a plan that was clearly working well, at least from his point of view.

It should have been a huge relief to exit the cabin, but after what I'd learnt, I left it with a sorry sense that nothing would ever be the same again. In some ways, it felt like life would have been much simpler if I'd stayed locked behind that door rather than having to walk through it and face the reality that was waiting on the other side of it. It was a reality that I knew would involve Grace having to face the music for the sins of her past once Joshua and Kamilla had engineered it so she became trapped in the cabin, which was simple enough because all they had to do was hide out of sight when Grace got home, and it was inevitable that she would go to look in the cabin once she saw that the door was open.

But even once Grace was locked inside the cabin and staring hopelessly through the window at me and her captors, I had been hoping that somehow, there was another explanation. What if, despite the evidence, Joshua, Kamilla, and Rosie, a woman I hadn't met but who was no less involved in this crazy plot, had all been wrong? What if Grace was innocent, and it was all one big misunderstanding? If it was, maybe there was a chance at salvation, for one of us at least. But it was not to be, as I listened in horror as Grace shouted down the phone and confessed to her crime, one that was recorded by a device Joshua had planted in there just after he had let me out.

With that taped confession, Grace knew she was screwed, and that was why she hadn't even bothered to try and run while Joshua called the police, and Kamilla glared at her with all the hatred of a woman who has had her family ruined. I watched on in dismay as my wife was handcuffed and taken into custody, just as Frank and Maggie, our nosey neighbours watched on, the pair of them standing outside their homes with troubled looks on their faces, looks that I'm sure were replicated once the full story broke in the media, and they got to read all about it in their newspapers at breakfast.

It's funny, but ever since it all happened, Frank and Maggie don't visit anymore. They seem to have lost their enthusiasm for knocking on our door and asking what we have been up to recently. At least one good thing has come from all this then, I suppose.

But that's about the best of it because once the truth was out, Grace had a lot of talking to do with the police. As the crime she had confessed to had occurred when she was ten years old, there was the chance for her to face punishment for it. If only she had been a few months younger, there would have been little that the police could have done because any crimes committed by someone under the age of ten in the UK are not prosecutable. But over ten and there is a small list of things that can be punishable, and one of those is murder.

While a lawyer did his best to get Grace to say she had no intention of killing her dad or Amy and that it was an accident that death occurred as a result of her locking the door, Grace actually dismissed that notion and told the police that she knew exactly what she had been doing. She admitted that despite her tender age, she had been fully aware that two people could not live for very long without access to food and water and that the longer she kept them in there, the more likely it was that they might die. It was a shocking admission, but it seemed to be one that Grace needed to get off her chest, perhaps only because carrying the guilt for all those years had left her wanting to own her sin rather than try to excuse or downplay it.

The result of the investigation and full confession for Grace, who, by the end of it was completely remorseful and entirely passive in the hands of the police, was that my wife, the woman I had married because I thought she was the finest person in the world at the time, was mentally unstable and required psychiatric help after an assessment deemed her dangerous to the public.

In reality, Grace is only dangerous to people she is close to, and even then, the danger only occurs when those people hurt her. That was her father's mistake, and that was mine too. But even so, Grace said she constantly entertained thoughts of locking people up and had a desire for controlling people, and even though part of me felt she said that to avoid having to start again in the outside world, her assessor said she required around-the-clock supervision and help. That was why she was sent to a psychiatric ward, and that is where she resides to this day.

In the end, it took a lot less effort to take apart the cabin than it did to construct it, and by the time the last piece of timber has been removed from my garden, all I'm left looking at is a large, dead patch of grass that the structure once stood upon. It's grass that died because it went too long without nourishment, and it's not dissimilar to the fate that befell poor Grace's dad and his mistress. It's also a fate that was very nearly my own, although I wasn't actually as close to it as I thought at the time.

Kamilla had a secret, just like Grace did, and ultimately, I've just proven to be a clueless, naïve man who has had his life turned upside down by women who knew better. I guess I could be forgiven for wanting to stay away from the opposite sex for a while now. But I'm not going to do that.

I may never see Kamilla again, and I most likely will never attract a woman her age again either. But there is one woman who still needs me, and I feel like in some small way, I need her too. I guess she needs me because she has requested that I visit her at the ward tomorrow, and I have reluctantly said yes to that invite.

I'm going to go and see Grace tomorrow, and while I have no idea what she wants to say to me when I get there, I know that seeing her will give me the chance to apologise for hurting her. I'll do that because the truth is that if I had been a good husband, she wouldn't have locked that door, just like she wouldn't have locked that shed door if her dad hadn't hurt her too. She might be a little crazy, but there's no denying the men in Grace's life have let her down badly.

All I can do is say sorry for that and hope it gives at least one of us some closure.

The question is - will she accept that apology, or is closure not something she is looking for yet?

If it's the latter, what does she want?

EPILOGUE

GRACE

For a woman who has an alcoholic for a mother, I'd have thought me ending up in a place like this after confessing to a serious crime would have definitely given my mum the perfect excuse to drink herself into an early grave. But bizarrely, at least from my perspective anyway, recent events have been the catalyst for Mum giving up the demon drink and embracing the sober life once again. I know this to be a fact because I've seen her sober with my own eyes when she came to visit me yesterday.

I'd asked for her to be contacted in the hope that she might be willing to visit me and listen to my apology for what happened with Dad. But I had in no way expected her to accept that invitation. The fact she had was a good sign, but it was an even better sign when she had entered my room on this ward and looked the best that I had seen her looking in a very long time.

Her eyes were brighter than I could ever remember them being, and her skin was no longer pale and blotchy. It looked like she had been out in the sunshine, and more importantly, it looked like she had been feeding her body with something a little more nutritious than red wine. But it wasn't her appearance that shocked me the most. It was what she said to me once she had taken a seat beside my bed and looked me in the eyes.

She told me that what had happened had been her fault, not mine.

I'd found that hard to agree with at first because I'd been the one who had locked the shed door on Dad after all. But Mum had explained to me that if it hadn't been for her turning to alcohol to cope with the mystery of his disappearance, she would have most likely noticed that something was troubling her daughter and could have gotten it out of me instead of leaving me alone in my bedroom while she languished with the bottle downstairs.

It was obvious to me that Mum really believed that, even if I didn't think it was that simple, but it was for that reason that Mum had decided to stop drinking. As far as she was concerned, she had been doing it because life had been unkind to her, but after the truth had come about Dad's death, she felt it was her being unkind to me that had really caused it.

It was a huge relief to make up with my mother, and despite my life still being far from in a state that anyone else would envy, things are a little better for me now than they were in the past. At least I have one parent back. But a new day brings with it a new visitor, and today is the turn of my husband to make the walk into the ward. However, I'm not expecting our meeting to go quite as smoothly as the one with my mum went.

I've barely seen Dominic since that day in the garden when I finally told the truth. If anything, I've just been waiting to receive notice that he would like to divorce me, and I could hardly blame him for that. But I haven't been served with divorce papers yet, so technically, I'm still married, although I don't feel much like a wife as I sit here in this bed in a very bland room with not even a bunch of flowers for company. But my solitude ends when one of my nurses pokes his head in the door and tells me that my visitor is here.

I'm not sure it's going to make much difference, but I quickly brush my hair behind my ears to hopefully improve my appearance before my husband enters the room and sees me sitting in the bed. When he does, his expression softens, and despite whatever mood he may have come here in, he is unable to hide his surprise at seeing what I look like these days.

I'm hardly going to apologise for make-up being the least of my worries in here, but it is a shame to see a man who once looked at me like I was the most beautiful woman in the world now almost pity what I have become.

'Hi,' I say, gesturing to the empty chair by my bed. 'How have you been?'

Dominic takes a seat, and after his eyes have wandered over the entirety of this small and sparse room that I now call home, he answers me.

'I've been okay. You?'

'Not bad.'

I decide not to get into all the tests, psychoanalysis and therapy sessions I've endured since being here, nor all the endless nights of soul-searching as I've sat awake in this bed, staring out of the window and wishing my life had gone down a different path. One of the biggest things I've wished is that I never left school that day when I was ten. All I had to do was stay in that playground, and my whole life would have turned out differently. Dad and Amy would have finished having sex at the shed and gone back to their families, and I would never have known about their affair, meaning I might have grown up to be a normal person without any of the unbearable guilt on my shoulders. Or maybe it's not that simple, and no matter what I did, I was always destined to end up in a place like this, one way or another. I might have just been born with a screw loose and was destined to turn out crazy. Either way, it's far easier to tell Dominic that I've been "not bad" than tell him all of that.

He asks me briefly about whether or not I feel this place is helping me, and I say that I think it is, although I'm unsure to what level all the medication I am on here has something to do with that. I feel drowsy and lethargic all the time, a far cry from the woman who had the energy to lock people in rooms, but perhaps that's supposed to be the point.

'Guess what?' Dominic says just as our basic conversation is in danger of petering out. 'The cabin has gone. It was taken apart yesterday.'

'Your man cave is no more?'

'I'm afraid not.'

'Hallelujah.'

Dominic can't help but laugh at my reaction to the demise of his precious cabin, though in reality, I'm a little sad to hear it has been dismantled. For him to willingly get rid of it must mean that it has forever been tainted beyond repair in his mind, and there must have been no way he could have ever foreseen himself being able to relax in there again. That's a shame because despite what he did inside it with Kamilla, in a way he was set up just as much as I have been, and if I was able to fall for it, I can hardly hold a grudge for him falling for it too.

'What a pair we are,' I say to try and lighten the mood a little more, but Dominic doesn't smile or say anything. He just keeps looking around at this place and at what our marriage has become. Visitations. Nurses. And ironically, locked doors, because ultimately, I've been deemed not fit to leave this place, so I can't just walk out without permission.

Unless I had a key, of course. Then I could get out. A key like the one on the nurse who takes me outside for exercise at 2pm each day. We just go for a walk around the enclosed courtyard, and while it's not much, it is nice to be in the fresh air. But it would be even nicer to be able to go home and be with my husband again, so that's why, after he has left me and I'm getting ready for my next bout of exercise, I entertain an idea. It's the idea of taking the nurse's key and using it to get out of here. But to do that, I'd have to distract the nurse. Maybe I could grab the key just as we're leaving the courtyard, and when I have it, I could lock her out while I'm on the inside. Then all I would have to do is walk through the building and out the front door. Sure, me getting out of here would mean locking somebody else up, a thing I have promised to never, ever do again.

But one more time can't hurt, can it?

THE END

Download My Free Book

If you would like to receive a FREE copy of my psychological thriller 'Just One Second', then you can find the link to the book at my website *www.danielhurstbooks.com*

Thank you for reading *The Couple In The Cabin*. If you have enjoyed this psychological thriller, then you'll be pleased to know that I have several more stories in this genre, and you can find a list of my titles on the next page. These include my bestselling book *Til Death Do Us Part*, which has a twist that very few people have been able to predict so far, and *The Intruder*, which became the #1 selling psychological thriller in the UK in September 2022.

ALSO BY DANIEL HURST

TIL DEATH DO US PART
THE PASSENGER
WE USED TO LIVE HERE
THE INTRUDER
THE BREAK
WHAT MY FAMILY SAW
THE RIVALS
WE TELL NO ONE
THE WOMAN AT THE DOOR
HE WAS A LIAR
THE BROKEN VOWS
THE WRONG WOMAN
NO TIME TO BE ALONE
THE TUTOR
THE NEIGHBOURS
RUN AWAY WITH ME
THE ROLE MODEL
THE BOYFRIEND
THE PROMOTION
THE NEW FRIENDS
THE ACCIDENT

(All books available now on Amazon and Kindle Unlimited – read on to learn a little more about selected titles…)

TIL DEATH DO US PART

What if your husband was your worst enemy?

Megan thinks that she has the perfect husband and the perfect life. Craig works all day so that she doesn't have to, leaving her free to relax in their beautiful and secluded country home. But when she starts to long for friends and purpose again, Megan applies for a job in London, much to her husband's disappointment. She thinks he is upset because she is unhappy. But she has no idea.

When Megan secretly attends an interview and meets a recruiter for a drink, Craig decides it is time to act. Locking her away in their home, Megan realises that her husband never had her best interests at heart. Worse, they didn't meet by accident. Craig has been planning it all from the start.

As Megan is kept shut away from the world with only somebody else's diary for company, she starts to uncover the lies, the secrets, and the fact that she isn't actually Craig's first wife after all...

THE PASSENGER

She takes the same train every day. But this is a journey she will never forget…

Amanda is a hardworking single mum, focused on her job and her daughter, Louise. But it's also time she did something for herself, and after saving for years, she is now close to quitting her dreary 9-5 and following her dream.

But then, on her usual commute home from London to Brighton, she meets a charming stranger – a man who seems to know everything about her. Then he delivers an ultimatum. She needs to give him the code to her safe where she keeps her savings before they reach Brighton – or she will never see Louise again.

Amanda is horrified, but while she knows the threat is real, she can't give him the code. That's because the safe contains something other than her money. It holds a secret. *A secret so terrible it will destroy both her's and her daughter's life if it ever gets out…*

THE WRONG WOMAN

What if you were the perfect person to get revenge?

Simone used to be the woman other women would use if they suspected their partner was cheating. She would investigate, find out the truth and if the men were guilty, exact revenge in one form or another. But after things went wrong with one particular couple, Simone was forced to go into hiding to evade the law.

Having assumed a new identity, Simone is now Mary, a mild-mannered woman who doesn't raise her voice or get angry, meaning nobody would ever suspect her of being capable of the things she used to do for a living. But when she finds out that her new boyfriend is having an affair, it awakens in her the person she used to be. Plotting revenge, Mary reverts back to the woman she once was before she went on the run and became domesticated. That means Simone is back, and it also means that her boyfriend and his mistress are in for the shock of their lives.

They messed with her. *But they picked the wrong woman.*

THE WOMAN AT THE DOOR

It was a perfect Saturday night. *Until she knocked on the door...*

Rebecca and Sam are happily married and enjoying a typical Saturday night until a knock at the door changes everything. There's a woman outside, and she has something to say. Something that will change the happy couple's relationship forever...

With their marriage thrown into turmoil, Rebecca no longer knows who to trust, while Sam is determined to find out who that woman was and why she came to their house. But the problem is that he doesn't know who she is and why she has targeted them.

Desperate to save his marriage, Sam is willing to do anything to find the truth, even if it means breaking the law. But as time goes by and things only seem to get worse, it looks like he could lose Rebecca forever.

THE NEIGHBOURS

It seemed like the perfect house on the perfect street. ***Until they met the neighbours...***

Happily married couple, Katie and Sean, have plenty to look forward to as they move into their new home and plan for the future. But then they meet two of their new neighbours, and everything on their quiet street suddenly doesn't seem as desirable as it did before.

Having been warned about the other neighbours and their adulterous and criminal ways, Katie and Sean realise that they are going to have to be on their guard if they want to make their time here a happy one.

But some of the other neighbours seem so nice, and that's why they choose to ignore the warning and get friendly with the rest of the people on the street. *And that is why their marriage will never be the same again...*

THE TUTOR

What if you invited danger into your home?

Amy is a loving wife and mother to her husband, Nick, and her two children, Michael and Bella. It's that dedication to her family that causes her to seek help for her teenage son when it becomes apparent that he is going to fail his end of school exams.

Enlisting the help of a professional tutor, Amy is certain that she is doing the best thing for her son and, indeed, her family. But when she discovers that there is more to this tutor than meets the eye, it is already too late.

With the rest of her family enamoured by the tutor, Amy is the only one who can see that there is something not quite right about her. But as the tutor becomes more involved in Amy's family, it's not just the present that is threatened. Secrets from the past are exposed too, and by the time everything is out in the open, Amy isn't just worried about her son and his exams anymore. She is worried for the survival of her entire family.

HE WAS A LIAR

What if you never really knew the man you loved?

Sarah is in a loving relationship with Paul, a seemingly perfect man who she is hoping to marry and start a family with one day, until his sudden death sends her into a world of pain.

Trying to come to terms with her loss, Sarah finds comfort in going through some of Paul's old things, including his laptop and his emails. But after finding something troubling, Sarah begins to learn things about Paul that she never knew before, and it turns out he wasn't as perfect as she thought. But as she unravels more about his secretive past, she ends up not only learning things that break her heart, but things that the police will be interested to know too.

Sarah can't believe what she has discovered. But it's only when she keeps digging that she realises it's not just her late boyfriend's secrets that are contained on the laptop. Other people's secrets are too, and they aren't dead, which means they will do anything to protect them.

RUN AWAY WITH ME

What if your partner was wanted by the police?

Laura is feeling content with her life. She is married, she has a good home, and she is due to give birth to her first child any day now. But her perfect world is shattered when her husband comes home flustered and afraid. He's made a terrible mistake. He's done a bad thing. *And now the police are going to be looking for him.*

There's only one way out of this. He wants to run. *But he won't go without his wife…*

Laura knows it is wrong. She knows they should stay and face the music. But she doesn't want to lose her man. She can't raise this baby alone. *So she agrees to go with him.* But life on the run is stressful and unpredictable, and as time goes by, Laura worries she has made a terrible mistake. They should never have ran. But it's too late for that now. Her life is ruined. The only question is: *how will it end?*

THE ROLE MODEL

She raised her. Now she must help her…

Heather is a single mum who has always done what's best for her daughter, Chloe. From childhood up to the age of seventeen, Chloe has been no trouble. That is until one night when she calls her mother with some shocking news. There's been an accident. *And now there's a dead body…*

As always, Heather puts her daughter's safety before all else, but this might be one time when she goes too far. Instead of calling the emergency services, Heather hides the body, saving her daughter from police interviews and public outcry.

But as she well knows, everything she does has an impact on her child's behaviour, and as time goes on and the pair struggle to keep their sordid secret hidden, Heather begins to think that she hasn't been such a good mum after all. *In fact, she might have been the worst role model ever…*

THE BROKEN VOWS

He broke his word to her. Now she wants revenge…

Alison is happily married to Graham, or at least she is until she finds out that he has been cheating on her. Graham has broken the vows he made on his wedding day. How could he do it? It takes Alison a while to figure it out, but at least she has time on her side. *Only that is where she is wrong.*

A devastating diagnosis means the clock is ticking down on her life now, and if she wants revenge on her cheating partner, then she is going to have to act fast. Alison does just that, implementing a dangerous and deadly plan, and it's one that will have far reaching consequences for several people, including her clueless husband.

WE USED TO LIVE HERE

How much do you know about your house?

When the Burgess family move into their 'forever' home, it seems like they are set for many happy years together at their new address. Steph and Grant, along with their two children, Charlie and Amelia, settle into their new surroundings quickly. But then they receive a visit from a couple who claim to have lived in their house before and wish to have a look around for old time's sake. They seem pleasant and plausible, so Steph invites them in. And that's when things start to change…

It's not long after the peculiar visit when the homeowners start to find evidence of the past all around their new home as they redecorate. But it's the discovery of a hidden wall containing several troubling messages that really sends Steph into a spin, and after digging deeper into the history of the house a little more, she learns it is connected to a shocking crime from the past. *A crime that still remains unsolved...*

Every house has secrets. But some don't stay buried forever…

THE 20 MINUTES SERIES

What readers are saying:

"If you like people watching, then you will love these books!"

"The books in this series are an incredibly easy read, you become invested in the lives of the characters so easily, and I am eager to know more and more. Roll on the next book."

THE 20 MINUTES SERIES (in order)

20 MINUTES ON THE TUBE
20 MINUTES LATER
20 MINUTES IN THE PARK
20 MINUTES ON HOLIDAY
20 MINUTES BY THE THAMES
20 MINUTES AT HALLOWEEN
20 MINUTES AROUND THE BONFIRE
20 MINUTES BEFORE CHRISTMAS
20 MINUTES OF VALENTINE'S DAY
20 MINUTES TO CHANGE A LIFE
20 MINUTES IN LAS VEGAS
20 MINUTES IN THE DESERT
20 MINUTES ON THE ROAD
20 MINUTES BEFORE THE WEDDING
20 MINUTES IN COURT
20 MINUTES BEHIND BARS

20 MINUTES TO MIDNIGHT
20 MINUTES BEFORE TAKE OFF
20 MINUTES IN THE AIR
20 MINUTES UNTIL IT’S OVER

About The Author

Daniel Hurst lives in the Northwest of England with his wife, Harriet, and considers himself extremely fortunate to be able to write stories every day for his readers.

You can visit him at his online home www.danielhurstbooks.com

You can connect with Daniel on Facebook at www.facebook.com/danielhurstbooks or on Instagram at www.instagram.com/danielhurstbooks

He is always happy to receive emails from readers at daniel@danielhurstbooks.com and replies to every single one.

Thank you for reading.

Daniel

THE COUPLE IN THE CABIN by Daniel Hurst published by Daniel Hurst Books Limited, The Coach House, 31 View Road, Rainhill, Merseyside, L35 0LF

Made in United States
North Haven, CT
06 January 2023

30680457R00167